MORE CLUES TO THE EXCITEMENT ABOUT

ROBERT BARNARD

"Barnard is an amusing Englishman
with an eye for the self-delusion and hypocrisy in all of us...
and the result is a growing series of mysteries that are
entertaining, often quite funny...and acutely observing."
—*The Boston Globe*

"A malicious gusto certain to amuse."
—*The Atlantic Monthly*

"Delightfully witty, deliciously satiric...An impudent,
devilish writer who leaves you begging for more."
—*The Buffalo News*

"Another triumph...scathing send-ups of literary world
pretensions...thoroughly satisfying work from an increasingly
commanding figure on the detection scene."
—*Kirkus Reviews*

"Hilarious!"
—*Minneapolis Star and Tribune*

DEATH OF A LITERARY WIDOW

Robert Barnard

A DELL BOOK

Published by
Dell Publishing Co., Inc.
1 Dag Hammarskjold Plaza
New York, New York 10017

First published in Great Britain in 1979 under the title
POSTHUMOUS PAPERS.

Dell® TM 681510, Dell Publishing Co., Inc.

ISBN: 0-440-11821-2

Reprinted by arrangement with Charles Scribner's Sons

One Previous Dell Edition
New Dell Edition
First printing—August 1985

CONTENTS

CHAPTER I

TWO OLD LADIES, LOCKED . . .

'That's my old girl,' said Greg Hocking, gazing out of the window of the Saloon Bar of the Spinners' Arms.

The bottom half of the window was frosted, and the new landlord, small and round, had to stand on tiptoe to see over it. Coming out of the gate in the high wall some way up the road, he saw a little old lady in a brick-coloured coat and a perky hat which had an air of defiance about it. Shutting the gate briskly, she turned and walked in their direction.

'She a regular?' he asked.

'Not what you'd call regular. She'll be in for a sherry or a gin-and-it two or three mornings a week. And sometimes she'll pop down for an hour on Saturday nights, if she's not with her daughter. Spry old character, isn't she?'

The landlord looked at the determined little figure, forging her way past his pub on the other side of the road, but his eyes—trained to distinguish beer drinkers from shorts drinkers, and trouble-makers from peaceful souls—saw nothing interesting in her. He turned to go back to his bar.

'Wait,' said Greg Hocking. 'You'll see the other come out within ten minutes, I'll bet you.'

They stood at the window in companionable silence, alone in the bar. The regulars at the Spinners' were not rushing along to make the acquaintance of the new landlord, for fear he should

get above himself. A canny lot, the people of Oswaldston. Greg Hocking, sipping his half pint, let his
warm brown eyes rove among the people scurrying
backwards and forwards in the street. Twenty
minutes to go before teaching began again. When the
gate up the road opened again, he gave a grunt of
achieved prophecy.

'That's her,' he said.

The second old lady was a very different figure: she
was substantial, imposing, must even in her time have
been voluptuous. Her clothes announced emphati-
cally that they were not chain-store products: a full,
beige cape swirled abundantly round her full figure
and was topped by a simple pudding-basin hat of
brown velvet, with a massive shady brim. She was a
model of style for the elderly, and to complete the
picture she had on a bright red lead a sprightly black
poodle. In earlier days, Hocking guessed, she would
have sailed forward with the splendid confidence of a
fine woman. Now she seemed to have trouble with
her ankles, and she walked carefully, seeming all the
time to be chafing against her carefulness.

The landlord watched her go slowly past. 'What's
so special about them two?' he asked.

'They're both going shopping,' said Greg Hocking,
seeming not to answer him, and watching the figure
on her way down towards the High Street. 'They
both live in that big old barn, her downstairs and my
old lady upstairs, and they each do their own shopping, separately, every morning, regular as clockwork.'

'Old people are funny sometimes,' said the landlord, finding it hard to maintain interest.

'They each do their own cooking, too, in the one
kitchen. Madam you've just seen has dinner in the
evening. My old girl has dinner midday. Breakfasts
can be difficult, I've heard, but mostly Madam sleeps

late. Otherwise they just listen for each other in the kitchen.'

The landlord went back behind his bar, oppressed by these domestic details, and began polishing glasses with shoe-black thoroughness, in readiness for when the vicinity honoured him with their company.

'Why do you say *your* old girl?' he asked, just to keep the conversation going.

'Oh, they're both my old girls really,' said Greg Hocking, turning his frank, smiling young face in his direction for a moment. 'But Hilda is my particular girl. I got talking to her in here—it was my first day in Oswaldston, and I was feeling lonely. Next time she saw me she asked me in for a cuppa, and we had a good old yarn. I always go round once or twice a week now to see they're all right.'

'Is she some sort of companion?' asked the landlord, holding a glass up to the light. Greg Hocking let out a splendid, ringing laugh.

'Not on your life! No, they hardly speak to each other from what I can gather. Only time I saw them together they started getting at each other, through me. Oh no, Hilda wouldn't be anybody's *companion*, not her!'

He paused, drinking meditatively, then he said: 'You could say they're related in a way, only we don't have a word for it. They were both married to the same chap.'

'By gum!' said the landlord, impressed enough to pause in his polishing. 'That's a rum set-up. Never heard that one before. Both ex-wives, eh?'

'Well, let's say one ex-wife and a widow,' said Greg Hocking. 'My old girl's the ex-wife. Except some say they were never really married at all. I wouldn't know about that. Ah—here she comes now, with her sausages and fish fingers.'

The landlord watched the little brick-coated figure

with a slight accession of interest as she trailed past
his window. There is something in an old scandal
which makes even the most torpid average human
being twitch his nose with interest. 'Poor old bugger,'
he said. 'Past it now, I'd guess.'

'Not a bit of it,' said Greg Hocking, annoyed and
protective. 'Game as they come, I shouldn't wonder.'

'But why do they live together?' asked the landlord.
'Sounds like a bloody awful arrangement to me.'

'Search me,' said Greg Hocking. 'But it's not awful.
They enjoy themselves no end, I can tell you that.
Why, only the other day I was talking with my old—'

But he was interrupted by the Saloon Bar door
being pushed tentatively open. Through it, slowly
and painstakingly, came the imposing figure in the
beige cape, preceded by the little black poodle, high-
stepping it over to the bar as if he were an Arab stal-
lion at an imperial review.

'Ah, good morning, Mr Hocking,' said its owner,
condescendingly.

'Good morning, Mrs Machin,' said Greg Hocking.

'A half bottle of gin, landlord,' said Mrs Machin,
her voice loud and confident, contrasting with her
ankles.

When she had been served, and had paid with a
five-pound note, flourished commandingly across the
bar, Mrs Machin turned back towards the door. But
before she got there she stopped, and looked at Greg
Hocking.

'I wonder,' she said, 'if I might trouble you to call
on me some time?' As she said it, her words were
something between a command and a request.

'Of course, Mrs Machin,' said Greg Hocking.

'Shall we say today, at tea-time, when you finish
teaching? Would that suit you, Gregory?'

It was the first time she had used his Christian
name. The landlord was amused to notice the

slightest flush of pink spreading up from the young man's neck.

'Of course, Mrs Machin,' he said again. 'That would suit me fine.'

'Very kind of you,' said the old lady. 'Come along, Pimpernel.' And preceded by her little dog, prancing like an enthusiastic chorus girl from a long-ago musical, she billowed out of the door, and crossed the road towards the gate of her house.

'She's a character, right enough,' said the landlord appreciatively. 'Been a tartar in her day, I'd guess.'

'And not just in her day, either,' said Greg Hocking.

'Got you where she wants you, I notice,' said the landlord. 'Why do you put yourself out? Just because she plays the grande dame doesn't mean you have to jump through the hoop when she snaps her fingers.'

'I like them,' said Greg Hocking. 'They interest me.' Then he added with a touch of pride: 'Anyway, they're something very special. In a month or two those two old dears will be known all over the country.'

The landlord stared at him for an explanation, but he drained his glass and walked out. He thought to himself that perhaps he had exaggerated a bit, but in fact the fame of the two widows Machin was in the next few weeks to exceed even his expectations.

CHAPTER II

THE SECOND MRS MACHIN

The town of Oswaldston was largely a product of the Industrial Revolution. Town histories and town guides talked of earlier times, but all physical trace of them had been swept away in the untrammelled pursuit of brass. If the centre of the town had once had character of a bluff, ruthless sort, it had been plastered down and trivialized in our own times: now it looked like any High Street of any not too prosperous town—a jungle of supermarkets and cheap chain stores, all with shrieking placards proclaiming phoney bargains and bogus price-slashing.

Meadowbanks, Viola Machin's house, was well over half a mile from the centre. It had been built over a century before by a mill-owner on the way up. It was of sandstone, grimed by the years, and though it had long since been overtaken by the town and become part of a mean little street of red-brick back-to-backs, it kept its head above them, and retained something of its old dignity and pre-eminence.

Mrs Machin's sitting-room was on the ground floor, one of four substantial, well-proportioned, satisfying rooms, all of them her domain. It looked out on to a walled wilderness of a garden and beyond that to the roofs of the working-class houses, dating back to the turn of the century. The furniture was not in period: it was mostly comfortable stuff from the 'thirties, tasteful, but a little soulless. The room was dotted

with small silver picture frames, each one holding a
snapshot that embalmed a fragment of Mrs Machin's
past. Greg Hocking would dearly have liked to in-
spect them, but he was chary of showing too lively an
interest in what he already thought of as the Machin
story, so instead he eased himself into the large
square armchair, which exhaled and received him in
a chintzy embrace.

Mrs Machin went serenely about the room, preparing the tea. Cups, milk and sugar she had laid already
on the coffee-table, with a well-loaded cake-stand, and
two plates of biscuits. The kettle was boiling on a
hot-plate in a dark little corner of the room (it had
been installed for convenience, and to avoid unnec-
essary clashes in the kitchen). She was wearing a
dark green woollen dress, fitting closely her still impressive figure. It was a poor comfort that people
should say she must once have been a fine figure of a
woman, but it was some comfort, and she exacted it.
It was nice to have a man in the house, she was
thinking. It didn't happen very often these days—
apart from her sons, and the vicar (but he didn't
count). She looked at Gregory Hocking sitting—
broad, open and healthy—in her armchair. Just finished Dip. Ed., something of a sportsman, enjoying
his first job and a regular pay packet. I could have
fancied you in my younger days, she said to herself.

Her conscious thought was—on this and many other
occasions—less than completely honest. She fancied
him now.

Finally, when the various stages of the ritual were
gone through, she placed the cosied teapot on the
tea-tray, cautiously settled herself in the other armchair, and, waiting for the pot to draw, looked expec-
tantly at her visitor.

'It's a very pleasant room,' said Greg Hocking,
feeling he was expected to start the ball rolling.

'It is, isn't it?' she responded graciously. 'The furniture, of course, is my own: I brought it with me when I married. It was, you know, my second marriage—' she paused, to barb the rest of the sentence to her own satisfaction—'as it was, *in a sense*, his.'

'I didn't know,' said Greg Hocking, neutrally.

'Oh yes. And in my own little way, I'd had a literary career of my own.' She leaned painstakingly over to the bookcase behind her, and pulled out three volumes, very conveniently to hand. The books still had their dustjackets on, but they were very dirty. One was an emaciated volume of verse, the next a collection of short stories, the last—larger, and illustrated—a cookery book: *The Cuisine of Australia and New Zealand*. She sat this last on her lap, and looked somewhat ruefully at it.

'It never sold very well, I'm afraid. In fact, I had difficulty in filling up the required number of pages. I was commissioned, you know. I was a very good cook, and I came from New Zealand. But it was a bit like the man—where is it?—who wrote the article on Chinese metaphysics by looking up "China" and "metaphysics" in the encyclopaedia and putting them together.' She looked at Greg Hocking to see if he was following, and seemed pleased that he was.

'I didn't know you were a New Zealander either,' he said, smiling back at her.

'I *was*,' she said, beginning to pour tea. 'I left as a gel, you know. It's hardly more than a memory now, and I never, luckily, had much of the accent. It's so easy, isn't it, to get labelled?' She handed him tea, and plied him with both plates of biscuits. 'I came to London in nineteen-thirty, intending—how odd to think of it now—to be a writer.'

'And instead of that, you married one,' said Greg Hocking, genially crunching a ginger nut.

'To be precise, I married *two*,' said Mrs Machin,

leaning back in her chair in an attitude of self-satisfaction. 'Silly thing to be proud of, but I suppose it's
a sort of claim to fame. But the first was—' she waved
her hand—'*negligible*. And Walter I had, alas, for
only two years. And by that time his writing life was
virtually at an end.' She looked at Greg Hocking intently, and he was struck by the hardness of her eyes:
even when talking of her husband's death, her main
emotion seemed to be that she had been defrauded of
something. 'His health, you know, deteriorated after
the war. For the last year of our marriage I was
merely a sick-nurse. It was the tragedy of my life.
There's a cliché, but how completely true it is! I
never got over it. I never wanted myself to write
again.' She looked ahead at nothing with tragic
blankness, like a rep actress in a late Ibsen play:
'Nothing—nothing—has had any meaning for me
since that day in nineteen-forty-eight when he died.'

Greg Hocking could think of no appropriate response so he cleared his throat, took a sip of tea, and
then said: 'But this new revival of interest in him
must be a great pleasure for you.'

Mrs Machin's mood changed, as at the drop of a
switch. 'Ah, yes. It's quite wonderful. A new zest.
Something to live for. A real Indian summer, just
when I was looking forward to nothing but—the
grave!' She seemed to consider her words too egotistical, for she leaned forward over the cake-stand, and
said: 'For *his* sake. It's wonderful that *he* will get the
recognition he deserved. Because he never really had
it, you know, never. It's not just that he was forgotten
after he died, as so often happens. He didn't even get
it in his own lifetime.'

'Really? I assumed he did, because people know his
name around here. And he had two books published,
didn't he?'

'Published, yes. And *The Factory Whistle* went into

three editions in nineteen-thirty-nine. But publication is not recognition. His other novel, you know, was never published. Simply never published. It has remained upstairs in the attic all these years, until now, when Mr Kronweiser is transcribing it.'

She raised her eyes heavenwards, as if Mr Kronweiser were some kind of recording angel. 'You know Mr Kronweiser?' she asked, bringing them back to her visitor.

Greg Hocking put down his cup, to give himself a pause. 'I have seen him a couple of times, in the Spinners' Arms. I suppose he was . . . soaking up atmosphere.'

Mrs Machin relaxed a little from the tensions of her tragic memories. 'He is very earnest,' she said, smiling faintly. 'Just the tiniest bit . . . *dull*. So *American*, too!' She leaned forward, and her smile now was something almost intimate. 'To tell you the truth, he's not my kind of man at all. As you can imagine, Walter's reputation being what it was! I find my sessions with him much less amusing than I had hoped. But of course I have to give him all the time I can. I have to share my memories with him. That much I feel I owe to posterity.'

The tragic muse seemed to have descended on her again, and Greg Hocking tried to relax the atmosphere by taking a piece of fruit cake and chewing appreciatively. 'Delicious,' he said.

'Shop,' said Mrs Machin dismissively. 'Much too moist. But it's not Mr Kronweiser I wanted to talk to you about today, Gregory. He sits up there, day in, day out, beavering away. No, I think I can trust Mr Kronweiser. It's these reporters . . .' She cast a look of great—but to him unfathomable—significance at Greg Hocking.

'Are they troubling you?' he asked—though he did not think that this was the matter he had been in-

vited to discuss. For an old lady, Mrs Machin gave
the impression that she was quite capable of dealing
with any intrusion or impertinence that mere reporters were likely to offer.

'No, no,' she said, smiling roguishly at his misunderstanding. 'I *like* them. They remind me of London, of—' she waved her hand theatrically—'the great
world. I was a sort of reporter myself, in my—salad
days, so I understand them very well, only too well.
That was in my very young days, by the way, before I
met my *first* husband.' She paused for a moment, and
then looked at him impressively. 'Of course, these are
not reports in *that* sense.'

'No?'

'Much more important. I should prefer to call
them writers who work on newspapers. Because of
course this is not going to be a "story" in the vulgar
sense.'

'Naturally not.'

'And there will be no sensationalism. The fact is,
the better papers have naturally got wind of what is
being talked about in the literary world.' There was a
heady whiff of Bloomsbury in the 'twenties about this
last phrase, and she looked to see if it had impressed
Greg Hocking. 'And there, people in the know are
naturally talking about my late husband. They know
his first novel will be reprinted next month, and the
book of stories later in the year. They know that Mr
Kronweiser is working on the manuscript of the second
novel, and that there is a mass of papers upstairs. It's
the sort of thing that naturally interests people.'

'Of course,' said Greg. 'It certainly interests me.'

'Kind of you to say so,' said Mrs Machin, beaming
on him condescendingly for his boyish enthusiasm.
'This has been in the wind for some time, you know.
The references to Walter have been piling up in the
last year or two. People send them to me—people I

once knew, in London, sometimes people quite out of the blue. There've been mentions in *Encounter*, the *New Statesman*, places like that. Now it's all coming to a head. He was a *very* significant working-class writer, and now he is going to have a big, a very big, revival!'

'That will be very exciting for you,' said Greg, feeling like a stuck-pig of a confidant. 'And I suppose the reporters are working on the background stuff?'

'Precisely. There will be a long article in the *Sunday Chronicle* colour supplement, and another in the *Sentinel* weekend review. And I'm afraid the *Sunday Grub* has got on to the story as well. Big fleas and little fleas, you know . . .'

She pulled herself up from her contemplation of future fame, and fussed around Greg in a hostessy manner. She poured him another cup of tea, pressed him to take another slice of cake, and generally behaved as something between mother and mistress. But he could see that her mind was still on the subject of Walter Machin's future recognition, and he said:

'All this will be very good for sales.'

'Very good! After all these years without a penny, I shall actually receive royalties. Quite a lot, too! I am going to make a *very* good deal for the second one, when the transcription is complete.'

'I suppose Mr Kronweiser—'

'Mr Kronweiser is transcribing the novel as part of his academic work on my late husband. That was agreed when he was given access to the papers. There is no question at all of his receiving remuneration for his labours.'

'Naturally not,' murmured Greg, cowed by the polysyllables.

'But it's not money, not money at all that interests me,' said Mrs Machin, once more spreading herself out over her chair in her actressy pose and looking

straight into Greg's eyes with an expression of stage
sincerity. 'It's the truth I'm interested in—making
sure the public learns the truth!'

For some reason Greg Hocking amended her last
words in his own mind to 'my truth'. But he said:
'I'm sure if the reporters are the sort you say they
are—'

'Oh, they are. Except that rather dreadful little
man from the *Grub*, of course, and nobody will pay
serious attention to anything *he* writes. And
naturally, I've talked to them—endlessly!—and supplied them with photographs, and so on. I've been
just as co-operative with them as I have with Mr
Kronweiser.'

She paused. Greg Hocking sat, with his cup and
saucer in his large hand, waiting for the nub of the
matter. Mrs Machin looked ahead of her, this time
genuinely in thought, her mouth pursed up in a not
very pleasant expression.

'And of course Mr Kronweiser I can trust. Mr
Kronweiser I have completely under—complete trust
in. On the other hand, the reporters . . . the newspaper writers . . .'

Greg Hocking looked at her in some bewilderment,
because she seemed to be demanding something of
him. 'There's nothing you can do about what they
write,' he said feebly. 'Unless there's a question of
libel . . .'

'No, no-o-o,' she said, smiling condescendingly. 'Of
course, *I* realize that, Gregory. I'm a woman of the
world. No, what I was trying to say was . . . that
they've been talking to our friend Hilda upstairs.'

She looked at Greg significantly, but he let his eyes
go blank—the sort of expression he assumed when
being lied to by his pupils. He felt the situation was
getting too difficult for him to cope with, and was relieved to hear a determined scratching at the door.

He got up to open it, but Mrs Machin forestalled
him.

'No, no,' she said, rising painfully. 'It's Pimpernel.
He doesn't know you very well. I shouldn't like to
startle him.'

She got to the door a little uncertainly. Pimpernel
danced in, registered Greg's presence, and stood some
feet from his armchair, letting out high piercing
barks, like an ageing Queen of the Night. Greg Hocking had never liked poodles.

'There, darling, there, it's a *nice* man, a good
friend, nothing to *bark* at, there, there, darling . . .'

Mrs Machin soothed the quivering black bundle
with all the overwhelming force of her heavy mater-
nality. She seemed to register Greg's lack of sympathy,
for when she had sat down she said pathetically:
'He's all I have. Now the boys are grown up.'

Greg took a Marie biscuit, and made half-hearted
overtures. Pimpernel took his hysterical fury over to
the other armchair, sprang up into his mistress's lap,
and lay down eyeing Greg with his coal-black arrogant eyes.

'There's a love,' said Mrs Machin. 'Now, we were
saying—?'

'About Mrs Machin—'

'Oh yes—*Hilda* Machin. Now, I *know* what good
friends you are. And I appreciate your loyalty to her.
I do. Nothing could be further from my mind than to
say anything against Hilda. After all, we've lived together now, the two of us, for nearly ten years. I
think it says something, don't you? about—well, about
both of us. That it's been possible at all.'

It was on the tip of Greg Hocking's tongue to ask
why it had been done in the first place, but Mrs
Machin swept on.

'And of course, I can see why they want to talk to
her. Naturally. After all, she—lived with him for

many years. She knows things about him and his life and background that even I—' the voice cracked with the painfulness of the admission—'even *I* do not know. But . . .' It came out in a flood: 'I wonder what she is saying about me!'

Hocking could hardly stop himself from smiling. Mrs Machin, with the sharp, bird-like eyes of a born performer, noticed the corners of his mouth twitching, and assumed a deprecatory smile herself in sympathy.

'Yes, I realize it must seem ridiculous to you, Gregory. A silly old woman, worrying about battles long ago.' She swept aside his protests with her superb old arms. 'I can see how I must look to you. You're of an age not to worry what people say about you! But . . . you know, she's never forgiven me, never. If we . . . if we fight, as we do, just now and again, she still accuses me of . . . getting him away. Of stealing him.' She had by now recovered her confidence, and she straightened her shoulders and said grandly: 'Which is nonsense, of course. We were both mature people. We both knew exactly what we were doing, what we wanted.'

'But you don't want Hilda to be able to put her side of the story to the reporters?' said Greg brutally. Pimpernel, responding to his tone, let out several top A's and bared a couple of nasty little fangs.

'Quiet, love, quiet.' Mrs Machin leaned forward and put a hand on Greg's thigh. 'No, of *course*, Gregory, of *course* she must be allowed her say. That's understood. And naturally I realize she will not be so *entirely* discreet as I have been. Because she is not— forgive me—she is *not* what we used to call a lady. But—but I *don't* want her telling lies about me. She shouldn't be allowed to.' Her voice rose under the pressure of genuine egotistical emotion.

'What makes you think she would want to?'

'Oh come, Gregory.' Mrs Machin's expression and

tone were pitying. 'The abandoned wife, or whatever
she was, talking about "the other woman". That's
what I am in her eyes. Of course she'll say things to
the reporters, if she dares.'

'They might not print them.'

'They might not. Not the serious papers. But then
again, they have ways of suggesting things . . .'

'I realize that, Mrs Machin. But, again, I don't really see where I come in.'

'Well—' she smiled at him almost conspiratorially,
though he was far from sure he was going to con-
spire—'I thought, as you and Hilda are such *friends*,
you could perhaps just . . . drop into the conversation . . .'

'Yes?'

'. . . the word "libel". I mean, just casually, to
make her aware there is such a thing. And you know
I *am* willing, if she should say . . . some of the
things I think she might want to say . . . I *am*
willing to go to court. I have my name to protect.'

Mrs Machin subsided into silence, but suddenly,
drawing herself together, she leaned across the little
table and directed the whole force of her personality
at Greg Hocking in a gesture of appeal. It possessed
the whole of her big, full-breasted body, and Greg
had never felt from an old woman so overpowering a
sense of strength, seductiveness, sex. He could understand how Walter Machin was prised from little
Hilda's grip. For the second time that day, he flushed.

'You do see, don't you, Gregory, how horrible it
would be to spoil all this? Just when Walter, at last, is
going to get the fame he deserved but never got in his
own lifetime? And then for the whole thing to be—
soiled, by a sordid wrangle between two old women, a
slanging match between two crones, digging up a not
too edifying past. It would be too dreadful. And ridic-

ulous. The whole thing would be drowned in dirty laughs.'

She came to an end. Greg sat silent. Of course, there was nothing really he could do. And yet—what she said had appealed to him. It *would* be a pity. Just when Oswaldston's own writer was getting his long-delayed recognition. He'd been long enough in the town to look forward to this happening. And he did have a lot of respect for Hilda. For this one too, though not in the same way. He would hate to see them both deluged in public ridicule, the butt of smutty jokes in the Spinners' Arms. He looked up.

'I'll do what I can,' he said.

'Gregory, you are a true friend,' said Mrs Machin grandly, getting up as if the audience were at an end. Greg Hocking, relieved at his dismissal, nevertheless thought she might have observed the social niceties to make her purposes less blunt. Mrs Machin was clearly a woman used to using people, and casting them off when they had served their (or her) purpose.

'I'll do what I can,' he repeated, starting for the door. 'Of course I can't guarantee—'

'Naturally not, but coming from you . . . if you could just *warn* her—'

'I don't know about warning, but perhaps I might, as you said, just drop a word or two into the conversation, in a friendly sort of way.'

'Exactly. Just what I hoped. I can't say how much I appreciate this, Gregory.'

'I'm happy to be of service, Mrs Machin.'

'Oh come. I hope we're going to be good friends. Please do try and call me Viola.'

'I'm happy to be of service . . . Viola.'

She gave him a benign, null smile of visiting royalty, and attended by Pimpernel—conducting complicated flanking movements around his feet on abstruse principles of his own—she showed him into the hall.

'You won't go up now?' she whispered.

'It would look a bit . . . obvious,' he whispered in reply, feeling like a minor character in Gilbert and Sullivan.

'You're quite right,' she mouthed. 'Clever of you. Much better a little later.' She opened the door, and as she walked out into the sunshine, blinking, she said softly: 'You'll go far.'

She made it sound something between a prophecy and an invitation.

CHAPTER III

THE FIRST MRS MACHIN

On Saturday night, the best and bingiest glad-time of the week, the men of Oswaldston and their women-folk went to their clubs and pubs, filtered best bitter down into their fattening guts, and remembered the late 'fifties, when they were all young Arthur Seatons, when the world was full of beddable women and fightable men, and the fat pay packets gave you loot enough and more to buy a good time from Friday to Monday.

Alf Ackroyd, landlord of the Spinners' Arms, had his wife in to help, and a tough young chap in the Public, and when he had a moment he reflected to himself that the neighbourhood was coming round, and looked round the bar with satisfaction. His dream was to do the old place up, good and modern, and when it happened he would have more than enough time to stand and survey his dreamed-of green desert of plasticated leather, for the neighbourhood would desert to cosier, cheaper haunts.

Greg Hocking stood at the bar and wished he wasn't that most suspicious of characters in a pub—a local teacher. The staff of the local College of Further Education tried to pretend they were different from ordinary school teachers, but Greg knew that to the regulars they were stained indelibly by their profession. He surveyed cautiously the clientele of the Saloon Bar.

No Hilda yet, but there was still time for her to
pop in. Next to him, and not by coincidence, were
standing three new faces, though in fact one he had
seen briefly, while visiting at Mrs Machin's. Their
voices were not of Lancashire, nor were their man-
ners. They were, he had by now established, the
reporters—or the gentlemen who wrote for the newspapers.

The *Sunday Chronicle* writer was a fleshy young
man—well dressed, well fed, well built and well
pleased with himself, with some generations of good
living behind him. His shirt was broadly striped in
blue, and fitted closely his rounded contours. His suit
was smart, made by a goodish tailor, his face was full
lipped and boyish, and his accent was public-school,
modified to suit the times.

The *Sentinel* man wore a floppy polo-necked
sweater, though it was a warm May night; his hair
was dishevelled and he had stubble on his chin. His
shoes had not been cleaned since they were new, and
would not be till they were discarded. His accent was
public-school, modified to suit the times.

The *Grub* man was ratty. Just ratty. He stood apart
from the other two, a mite contemptuous.

They were talking about Viola Machin.

'She's an absolutely superb old thing,' said the
Chronicle. 'A real survival from another age. Of
course, she's over the roof-tops about all the publicity.
Pretends she's past caring except for Walter's sake,
but she's lapping it up. I say, old chap, we'd better go
through the photographs tomorrow. I'm writing the
story around them, and we ought to try not to duplicate.'

'Fair enough. I'll only want three or four. But we
may have to duplicate on the Hilda Machin one, the
one of them together at Filey, you know.'

'I know the one. Yes. She's been close, hasn't she?'

They shook their heads, as at the world's ingratitude.

'Has she only given you the one?' asked the *Grub*.

'Yes,' said *Chronicle* and *Sentinel* in unison.

'Oh,' said Ratty non-committally. The other two looked at him suspiciously, sipping their gins and tonic.

'I can understand old Viola not handing out happy snaps from the first marriage,' said *Sentinel* experimentally, 'but I can't see why our 'Ilda shouldn't be a bit more forth-coming. I thought the two were at daggers: a few happy snapshots would have suggested that poor old Walter was dragged away from our 'Ilda by a scheming woman.'

'Perhaps there *were* no happy snapshots,' said *Chronicle*, similarly tentative, and eyeing Ratty, who was looking into his beer and seemed to like what he saw. 'Perhaps there was no money for things like that. Depression and all that jazz. Perhaps they fought like cat and dog. Our 'Ilda has a mind of her own, I'd guess.'

'Actually, they weren't that hard up, or shouldn't have been,' said *Sentinel*. 'Our Walter was in work all through the 'thirties. Down at Mattingley's. Supervisor too. I don't suppose there's many around here could say the same.'

'I'm playing down the social angle,' said *Chronicle*, with a practised air of Etonian world-weariness.

'Are you? Why?'

'Our readers are fed up with paraded social consciences. Anyway, I know bugger all about it, and I'm not going to that grotty library to read it up. I'm concentrating on the personal angle.'

'I always said your paper was a poshed-up version of the *Sunday Express*,' said *Sentinel* genially, pushing back his hair from his eyes. He turned to the *Sun-*

day Grub man: 'I suppose you'll be doing the same, eh Bill?'

'Oh aye,' said Bill. 'I'll be doing that. But my piece will mostly be pictures.'

They looked at him dyspeptically. There were no playing-fields ethics in the lower reaches of Fleet Street.

'Anyway,' said *Sentinel,* 'I've got the first couple of paragraphs of the new book. Old Viola gave me permission, and I prised it out of that creepy Yank.'

'What a pill. Christ, what a human incubus. Viola sent me up to get a letter she wrote to Walter, just before the war ended. You'd have thought I'd asked for dirty books in the Vatican. Looks this way and that, shuffles and snuffles, says he doesn't really think . . . Finally I read him the Riot Act, and he handed over a typescript—a carbon copy, at that, and numbered and cross-indexed and all manner of nonsense. That's the trouble with these American researchers: they guard their discoveries like Pamela her virtue. And he's the worst specimen I've come across. Nasty, shifty bugger. Anyone would think he owned the manuscripts.'

'I say,' said *Sentinel,* 'perhaps he does. Perhaps his university's bought them. They do, you know.'

'But they haven't, old man. I asked Viola specially. American universities have fallen on hard times. Most of them have stopped buying second-rate authors' cast-off underwear. But old Kronweiser has been given the right to sort through the papers, and transcribe them, and he's taking every advantage of it he can.'

'Watch it. Here he is.'

The three Fleet Street heads swivelled and looked at the Saloon Bar door. It is difficult to look sinister wearing casual clothes, but Mr Kronweiser very nearly managed it. He was dressed in pale blue slacks,

pink and white check shirt, and sneakers, but he did
not look fresh, for Oswaldston grime or the labours of
the day had robbed his clothes of their glow, and
there were sweaty patches under the arms of the shirt.
Mr Kronweiser was pear-shaped, like a pregnant
crow, the way American men get with too sedentary a
job and too much junk food in their diet. His face
was red and unhealthy, not well shaven, and sur-
mounted by a mop of black hair, just beginning to
turn grey. Sadly, he was barely thirty, but the long-
knifed struggle for jobs, for tenure, for an impressive
list of publications, had aged him well beyond his
calendar years—and he had never been a young young
man. He walked, or waddled, stealthily, his eyes darting from left to right. His manner mixed false geni-
ality, false sincerity and natural shiftiness, a mixture
made familiar by American politicians. People slid
away as he made his way over to the bar.

Greg Hocking grunted a greeting to Mr Kronweiser, and louder, more spurious greetings came
from *Chronicle*, *Sentinel* and *Grub*.

'Hi,' said Mr Kronweiser, showing his teeth briefly
to each, 'hi, hi. A small lager, please. Cold.'

'Finished work for the day?' asked *Chronicle* genially.

'That's right,' said Mr Kronweiser.

'Interesting job you've got there.'

'That's so. If you gentlemen will excuse me . . .'
And Mr Kronweiser shuffled sideways with his glass to
a corner bench, took a gross American paperback
from his posterior trouser pocket, and pretended to
read. But Greg Hocking saw it was a pretence. He
turned over pages he had not looked at, and in fact
was very busy keeping his eyes and ears attuned to everything around him.

'Endearing little soul,' said *Sentinel* under his
breath.

'Beneath that Humpty-Dumpty exterior,' said *Chronicle*, 'there lurks a thoroughly tough egg.'

The shadow cast by the globular Kronweiser settled like smog over the bar for some minutes. It was only when the door was opened again that the atmosphere lightened. Greg Hocking heard some jovial 'Hello Hildas' and a cheery 'Hello my old duck', and his old girl came glad-handing it over to the bar.

'Half of stout, please, Alf,' said Hilda Machin, rummaging in her handbag.

'Let me, Mrs Machin,' said *Chronicle* and *Sentinel*, in ragged unison, diving for their wallets.

'Ee—I've never been so popular. No, thanks, boys, I'll buy my own this time round.'

She slapped down her money on the counter, and took a sup of her stout.

'Next time round, then,' said *Chronicle*.

'Happen,' said Hilda Machin, giving him a roguish look. 'But whatever it is you want, I'm not promising to give. I'm too old a hand to give her all for a half of stout, believe you me.' She turned to Greg Hocking and patted him on the arm. 'Anyway, I've got my best boy-friend here tonight, and he's better looking nor you two.' She stood on tiptoe and whispered into Greg's ear: 'Come and 'ave a chat in the corner, eh, love? I sometimes get the feeling these two are taking notes.'

Greg laughed, got up from his stool, and ushered her over to an empty corner table. He felt rather than saw the eyes of the reporters following him; but he certainly saw the dull, dark eyes of Mr Kronweiser half-rise from his paperback and register their move. He was nibbling his lips with irritation. Greg thought he was wishing he had chosen a nearer seat.

'You don't mind, do you, Greg?' said Hilda, as she took off her coat and settled herself in. He smiled rather than answered, and looked at her proudly.

Hilda Machin had little of Viola's Kensington smartness, but she had a love of bright colour, and it marked her off. Under her brick coat she was wearing a claret-coloured frock, and it, and her cheery bird-bright face, lit up the dusty corner of the Spinners' like a lamp in a dark place.

'They're a fine pair, those two,' said Hilda, nodding in the direction of *Sentinel* and *Chronicle*, who were feigning conversation. 'One of them dressed up like the dog's dinner, the other looking like something the cat's brought in, but both of them as like as two peas underneath.'

'Don't you like them?'

'I've no call, either way. They're Viola's little boys. She's got them tied around her apron-strings—"yes miss, no miss, three bags full, miss". I'm not poking my finger in. I've got my own little follower.'

'I thought as much,' said Greg, draining his pint and sitting back to watch her, amused. 'You've been doing deals with the *Sunday Grub*, haven't you?'

Hilda Machin followed his lead and took a significant swig of stout. Instead of answering him, she said: 'And what did Madam want you for yesterday?'

Greg was caught off his guard. 'Oh, er, just a chat, like,' he said. Hilda cackled at his discomfiture.

'I'll bet,' she said. 'And which role was Sybil Thorndike rehearsing for on this occasion?'

Greg, who was lighting a cigarette, bent over, coughing. 'Well,' he said when he straightened, feeling he owed no loyalty in that particular direction, 'there was a touch of Cleopatra.'

'Really?' said Hilda, raising thin but eloquent eyebrows. 'The serpent of the Nile celebrating her diamond jubilee? Well, she must have wanted something out of you. The last time I saw her doing that little act was with Walter. And she certainly wanted something out of *him*.'

'Can I get you another?' said Greg, grabbing up her glass and heading towards the bar.

'Need time to think, eh? Well, that's Hilda Machin: always loses her man by being too sharp.'

When Greg returned with her second stout and another pint for himself, Hilda Machin said: 'On consideration, I'll spare you the embarrassment of telling a lie.'

'Good,' said Greg, thinking she had given up.

'I'll tell you myself what she wanted. She wanted you to warn me off.'

'Warn you off?'

'The reporters. Don't act the wide-eyed innocent. You're not so green as you're cabbage looking. She wants to make sure the joyful resurrection of Walter Machin isn't marred by anyone hearing Hilda Machin's side of the story. Right?'

'Right,' said Greg, after a pause. Then, sounding weak even to himself, he said: 'And she has a point, you know. Otherwise I wouldn't have gone along with her. It would look pretty undignified, the two of you, slogging it out in print.'

'I've never gone in much for dignity,' said Hilda. 'Unlike Dame Sybil . . . So the great British public is only to hear dear Viola's side of the story of Walter Machin's first marriage, eh?'

'Well, put like that—'

'How else should I put it?'

'Actually, I think that she's tried to steer clear of the whole subject.'

'I don't wonder,' said Hilda Machin in a voice of doom. 'If I were her, I'd want to steer clear of it too.'

They both turned their attention to their glasses, and Hilda Machin's eyes had the air of looking down the long, cratered road of her own past. Greg was mentally kicking himself for reminding her of it, and perhaps for losing her trust. 'Of course, if she said anything that wasn't the truth . . .' he began, weakly, not quite knowing how to complete the sentence.

'Oh, the truth. The truth's the last thing likely to come out on these occasions, isn't it? I don't suppose *either* of us would much care for that. Still . . . I'm not sure that I like Walter Machin's first marriage being passed over as if it were something best left under the carpet. We were married nigh on ten years, you know.'

'Have you been talking to reporters?'

'Tweedledum and Tweedledee? Not on your life. We don't speak the same language.'

'But the man from the *Grub*?'

'Well, not to say talking,' said Hilda Machin, leaning back on her bench seat with an air of self-satisfaction. 'If you want to know the truth, I've hardly said a word to any of them, him included. If they get close to anything personal . . . "intimate" like . . . do you know what I say? I look them straight in the eye and say: "My lips are sealed." Just like that. I never thought that was something you could actually say, but you can!'

Greg smiled: 'Mrs Machin will be pleased.'

'Viola will, will she? Bully for her. Well actually, Greg, to come clean—well, more or less clean—I don't want to spoil things any more than she does. Tell you the truth, I'm looking forward to it no end. All I've done—'

'Yes?'

'—is to give my old photograph album to the *Grub* man. Poor little chap—fancy looking like that, eh? So he'll have a whole pageful of happy snaps. Walter and Hilda on their wedding day—ah, that caught you out; you didn't think I'd had one, did you? Walter and Hilda and the baby. The happy Machins at Blackpool. Walter, Hilda and Viola in Trafalgar

Square. That's a prize one, that is. The little *Grub*
man's eyes almost sparkled when he saw that one: big
Walter with his arm around little Hilda and not so
little Viola, grinning like a parliamentary candidate.
Very poignant I find that one.'

'And that's your way of giving your side of the
story, I suppose, is it?'

'You could say that. Nobody can object, as far as I
can see. Just a photographic record of Walter
Machin's first marriage. The camera cannot lie—well,
it can, but not half so much as Viola and me would,
given half the chance.' She cackled with merriment,
and then added: 'I got a packet for them.'

'Everybody,' said Greg Hocking, 'seems to be expecting to make a bit out of the Machin revival.'

'And why not? You sound like a mucky little Methodist. We made precious little out of him during his
lifetime.' Hilda's belligerence subsided quickly, and
she smiled slyly. 'Viola made even less than me, poor
duck. He was too ill to work after they'd been married no more than a year. He'd gone back to the mill
in 'forty-six, but he wasn't there long. So this'll be the
first time Viola's made anything out of him. It'll be
better than the government's Christmas bonus!'

'She has money herself, doesn't she? Private means,
as they say?'

'Viola? Oh yes. It was her money bought the
house.'

'I wonder she let him go back to the mill.'

'What do you think—? That they should have gone
to live in Bloomsbury and joined the London "you-
lick-my-arse" group? Walter would never have stood
for that lot. Quite apart from—other reasons. Anyway,
there was no question of her "letting" him go back to
the mill. Walter wasn't any woman's poodle. Walter
did what Walter wanted, and quite right too. From

what I hear she managed to get the upper hand later on, but by then he wasn't himself by a long chalk.'

'Tell me,' said Greg, changing the subject as abruptly as she had earlier, 'why you sometimes talk Lancashire and sometimes talk posh.'

She looked at him quickly. 'What's so surprising about that? We all can. You wouldn't know. You're from Cheshire. You're practically a Southerner.'

'Not everyone can do the posh as well as you.'

Hilda sat back, rolling her glass around the palms of her hands, and contemplated him. 'I'm not the mill-girl that married the foreman, you know. You thought I was, didn't you? Made it seem all "right and romantic", didn't it? Oh, I got an education in my time—better than Madam's, if the truth be known. She went to a finishing school in Switzerland, and the only use they have for books there is to walk around with them on their heads. That was the sum total of her higher education. After that she started sleeping with people who could be useful to her. But I went to Teachers' College.'

'I didn't know,' said Greg.

'That's what I was when I met Walter.'

'What—a teacher?'

'That's right. In fact—well, never mind. I never told you because you're all so snooty up at t'College. I taught the first three years we were married—until Rose came along. Then I gave up. It wasn't the done thing in those days to go on after you'd begun a family, not like now. I did a bit later on, though—in the war, and after Walter left me.'

'He left you, did he?'

'Well, shall we say never bothered to come back to me. Viola grabbed him in 'forty-six. I think she was handed over with his demob suit.'

'Was it a surprise?'

'Not altogether. Walter would never have made it

into the Festival of Light. And there was plenty
willing in the mill in those days. So it wasn't the first
time. And she'd been doing her big act for him since
way back in 'thirty-nine.'

'Did you resent it?'

'No—you know me. Sunny-natured Hilda. I said,
"Be happy, my children." And that's enough questions, Mr Nosey Parker Hocking. You're as bad as
those scribblers over there. There's me daughter.
There's Rosie.' She waved to a mist of fair hair over
by the door. 'We're going over to Blackburn for a bit
of a do. See you soon, Greg love. Ta-raa.'

'What message shall I give to Mrs Machin?' Greg
called after her, incautiously.

Hilda Machin stopped in her tracks and turned
round. 'You can tell Viola,' she said loudly, 'to keep
her hands off my young men.' And bursting into a
cackle of laughter she swooped on her daughter and
bore her out of the Spinners' in triumph.

Greg downed the rest of his bitter and was uneasily
conscious of several pairs of sharp Lancastrian eyes
on him. God knows what they're thinking, he said to
himself. He tucked his shirt in at the back, and began
to edge his way through the Saturday night crowd. As
he passed the newspapermen, he got a triple invitation to have another, but he put on his sunniest
smile, said two was his limit, and made it to the door.
As he walked down Parfitt Road towards the High
Street and the buses, breathing the modified freshness
of the night air of Oswaldston, he heard the Saloon
Bar door shut again, and in a moment he was conscious of a dark shadow gaining on him in the twi-
light.

'Hello, Mr Kronweiser,' he said, through the back
of his head.

'Oh, hi,' said Kronweiser awkwardly. Greg kept up

his normal speed, and the American's fat little legs had to go nineteen to the dozen to keep up.

'I wondered,' he said, puffing . . . 'did she promise?'

'Promise?' said Greg, not slackening. 'Promise what?'

'To . . . keep quiet. Not to stir up the shit.'

'How did you know I was going to ask her not to?'

'Oh, Viola, of course, that is, Mrs Machin. She said that you were going to.'

'Oh, ah, really? That's my bus. I must run for it. Good night.'

As Greg leapt on to the departing double-decker, the conviction sprang fully formed into his mind that during his conversation with Viola Machin, Mr Kronweiser had been listening at the door.

CHAPTER IV

THE NEW GENERATION

Viola Machin, seated in her bay window, watched from under hooded lids the approach of her daughter-in-law through the wall gate and up the garden path. Her elder son's wife was a long-standing irritant, like an ill-perforated toilet roll. She'd never known a woman, she thought to herself, who dressed so conventionally, whose face was more boringly nondescript, whose hairdresser performed such miracles of dreariness. She's the most uninteresting person I know, she said to herself, with considerable satisfaction.

'Hello, Mother,' said Margaret Seymour-Strachey.

'Hello, Margaret,' said Viola with a sigh. She seemed bored already by the visit.

'Desmond is parking the car,' said Margaret brightly.

'So I imagined,' said Viola.

She made no further efforts at conversation. She wondered why her daughter-in-law bothered to continue her visits. She had made her attitude clear enough to her, heaven knows, but here she was, still coming back every other Sunday, year after year, as welcome as the Irish potato blight.

She's really pleased to see us, thought Margaret Seymour-Strachey, but she's too proud to show it, poor old thing.

On the entry of her son Desmond, Viola Machin

brightened up ostentatiously. He was not her favourite son, but he was *something*. Thank God she'd only
had sons. She always preferred men in the house.
Poor old Hilda—lost out there, as in everything else!
She bustled round, putting on kettles and opening
tins of biscuits and cake. Desmond Seymour-Strachey
sat, accepting the bustle, as was his wont. In his early
forties, with a hawk-like profile, he was good-looking
enough, yet in a voracious, untrustworthy style that
warned people off, and injured him in his business.
He was something in insurance.

'Not long to the big day now, Mother,' he said.

'Publication day?' said Viola Machin, standing back
to survey a groaning cake-stand. 'No, not long.
They've brought it forward a little, so that it comes
out in the last week of April—after the newspaper
pieces. Two and a half weeks to go.'

'Perhaps you could have a little party on the big
day,' said Margaret brightly.

'I had thought,' said Viola, splendidly aloof, 'of
having a large one.' It was in fact the first time she
had thought of such a thing, and it did not seem to
be a very good idea, but nothing irritated her more
than being addressed in that Listen With Mother
voice (particularly as her daughter-in-law spoke to
her children quite normally) and it goaded her to
contrariness.

'Wouldn't it tire you?' said Desmond quickly. And
getting no response from Viola, who continued fuss-
ing over the teapot, he added, more directly: 'It
would be silly to blue the profits before they've even
begun to come in.'

'Yes,' chimed in his wife, who had sworn to love,
honour and echo, 'save it all up into a nice little nest
egg.'

Viola Machin, feeling herself once more subject to

a process of diminution, said loftily: 'It will not be a *small* nest egg.'

She kicked herself as soon as she had said it. She had a pretty shrewd idea that Desmond had only the haziest notion of how much could be expected from the various books, and she had intended to keep it that way. As soon as Desmond's boney nose sniffed money, trouble could be expected. He had left school at sixteen to make money. Failing that he had married money (little though one would think it, mused Viola, to look at her) and now that much of that was gone on an over-large house, over-large cars, and over-large meals, Desmond was back in the market-place, avid for a quick kill. To give him his due, he made no attempt to hide this consuming interest of his: it would have seemed pointless, for he assumed that everyone else was similarly obsessed, and would see through his attempts at concealment.

Now that Viola had let the cat out of the bag, she felt she had no option but to come clean.

'I expect to make a lot of money,' she said coolly, sitting down to pour. Her manner said that this was a thing of great indifference to her, but that she was just setting the record straight. 'With all this publicity, Jackson's is expecting *The Factory Whistle* to do very well. And they think the new one will be a best-seller. It should bring in a great deal of money.'

'He never made much out of them before,' said Desmond, sceptically, but with hope.

'Your stepfather was ahead of his time,' said Viola, with a romantic sigh. 'Anyway, they were published by Mattlock's, who had no more business sense than a rabbit. Thank goodness we're not in their hands any-more. Jackson's has bought the rights, and Jackson's could make a Coptic dictionary into a best-seller if they tried. Things are going to be very different in the future, I assure you.'

She handed Desmond his tea, and allowed her daughter-in-law to fetch her own. Then she went on, with considerable pleasure and anticipation in her voice: 'The American rights to the new one have been sold, and so have the English paperback rights— for a very large sum. *The Times* is putting one of the short stories into their Saturday Review. There is talk of a film of *The Factory Whistle*, with Alan Bates, and they are going to read it on the BBC too. There will be a lot of money . . .'

She paused dramatically.

'All of it, I shall keep control of. Do I make myself clear? I shall use it, or not use it, as I think fit.'

'Of course, Mother,' said Desmond, smiling unpleasantly.

'Naturally, Mother dear,' said Margaret sweetly. 'Nobody would think of trying to dictate to you.'

Desmond stirred his tea and ate a biscuit. There didn't seem anything to say: even Margaret was nonplussed, and the air of the room was musty with unspoken thoughts. And the unspoken thoughts were all about money. At last, just to hear his own voice, Desmond said: 'Funny, I never could imagine Walter Machin writing books, let alone good ones.'

It was not a tactful remark.

'You didn't know him,' said his mother contemptuously.

'I knew him well enough,' said Desmond, on the defensive. 'I was nearly ten when you married him, remember.'

'Ten!' said Viola Machin.

'I knew him better than I knew my own father, anyway.'

'Obviously, since you never saw your own father after the age of six. Except that—I gather—you have been renewing the acquaintanceship recently.'

'That's right,' said Desmond, not apparently

ashamed, but not pursuing the subject. 'But old Walter, he was such a jolly soul—so bright, and loud, and down-to-earth, so much the life and soul of the party. Not at all my idea of a writer.'

'I believe Charles Dickens was generally considered a very lively companion,' said Viola, at her most distant. She laid her cup on the table, and leaned back in her chair, her statuesque pose accentuated by the classic fawn dress and the dark green scarf around her throat. She closed her eyes theatrically, and resembled nothing so much as a reigning prima donna who is being pestered by her producer to act. Margaret Seymour-Strachey, sensing the royal displeasure, hastened to undo the mischief.

'Of course your mother is quite right,' she said, with her cranked-up cheerfulness. 'Writers come in all shapes and sizes. I've met lots at the Blackburn Literary Club. Some of them seemed really perfectly ordinary!'

'No doubt,' said Viola, opening her eyes a fraction to peer malevolently from under the slits. 'These days the world is full of perfectly ordinary writers. But Walter Machin was *not* ordinary though he *was* funny, and lively, and good company—as well as being a great and shamefully neglected novelist.'

'He was wonderful with his hands, too,' said Desmond ingratiatingly. 'Nothing was a problem to him, I remember. He could mend any broken toy, and make things too—I remember he made a great big rocking-horse for Hilary, and painted it in all sorts of marvellous colours. And he did wonderful things with my clockwork trains that I never thought of doing.'

'You're right, of course,' said Viola, unfreezing a fraction. 'He was the poet of work—that's what the man from the *Sentinel* called him. He was wonderful on *things*, on everyday smells and sounds, and what it *felt* like to work with your hands. He could make you *feel* machinery. D.H. Lawrence couldn't make you feel that, because he'd never been a worker. But Walter had, and anyone who has read the books can feel it.'

Viola Machin looked even more aristocratic than usual as she expatiated on Walter Machin as working-class novelist.

'Yes, that's the sort of thing I remember about him,' said Desmond, adopting sycophancy as the easiest way out. 'And the time when he was ill I hardly remember at all.'

'And yet he was up there for nearly a year,' said Viola, casting eyes heavenwards again, like Mr Stiggins speaking of rum. 'And we'd only had a few months of marriage.'

'But those must be the months I remember so well,' said Desmond. 'Though of course there was also that long leave he had towards the end of the war.'

There was a doom-laden pause, and Desmond became conscious he had said the wrong thing again. Viola fixed him with her most commanding stare: '*Much* better not to mention that,' she said.

Desmond looked nonplussed: 'Oh yes of course, if you . . . I suppose our Hilda might . . .'

'Exactly. She might be hurt. It might get into the papers, and then she'd be down here knocking on my door and screaming blue murder. No better not give her any excuse to make that sort of trouble. *Much* better forget it altogether.'

'How is our Hilda?' asked Margaret Seymour-Strachey. All the children called her 'our Hilda', though in fact Desmond and Margaret had not spoken to her more than once or twice in their lives.

'Well, I believe,' said Viola, with her usual loftiness when that name was mentioned, 'enjoying her little part in the great events. I had to convey to her a slight warning, though . . .'

'A warning?'

'With so many reporters around, I thought she might be tempted to rake up old scores. She's a loose-tongued, prattling creature, like most women of her class. I decided it was best to avoid trouble, rather than face it when it comes. I will *not* consent to be portrayed in the press as a superannuated scarlet woman!'

Unseen by Viola Machin, something very close to a smile wafted over her daughter-in-law's face.

'And did she—heed the warning?' asked Desmond.

'I have reason to believe she saw the sense of it,' said Viola. 'I don't think we need anticipate any nonsense from *that* quarter.'

'You don't think it might have been better to let her have her say out,' suggested Desmond, 'and get it off her chest? Instead of trying to silence her?'

'Silence her!' said Viola Machin, her cheeks puffing with annoyance. 'What an extraordinary expression! Whatever could make you think I wanted to silence Hilda Machin? Even if I did, I don't see how I could silence her. Do you, Desmond?'

There was a long silence. The Sunday visit, frosty from the beginning, now seemed positively to crackle.

'I saw Father on Wednesday,' said Desmond finally, desperate for something to say.

'Indeed? And how was he looking?'

'Wonderfully fit. He is awfully well preserved.'

'He would be. He always took very good care of himself.'

'From the look of you, Mother,' said Desmond ingratiatingly, 'most people would say you were pretty good at that yourself.'

'It is natural for a woman to take good care of herself,' said Viola Machin, superbly secure in her right to generalize about women. 'In a man it is mere effeminacy. I have no desire to see Gerald playing the handsome patriarch.'

'What a pity, Mother. I was rather wondering if we might not arrange a meeting. He said himself he was very keen to see you again.'

'Really?' said Viola, her eyebrows flying theatrically up, though not with any apparent pleasure. 'Whatever can have put that notion into his head? Perhaps he wants to propose to me again.'

'Goodness, Mother,' said Margaret Seymour-Strachey, 'what can have given you that idea?'

'There are precedents.'

Margaret Seymour-Strachey's conventional bourgeois soul seemed shocked by the notion. Her husband merely said: 'He didn't say anything about that. He seemed very comfortable.'

The possible implications of this last remark struck Desmond himself as he was making it, and they were certainly not lost on Viola, who compressed her lips together grimly.

It seemed time to go. In perfect unison, based on long marital experience and an infinitesimal twitch of the eyebrows, Desmond and Margaret Seymour-Strachey rose from their chairs and began making the ritual noises.

'Well, Mother, we'll see you in a fortnight's time.'

'Perhaps then,' said Viola, whose lips were still set in a Gladstonian expression, 'you will find it possible to bring my grandchildren along for me to have a look at.'

Margaret Seymour-Strachey (who prided herself on being the perfect daughter-in-law) would do anything for her husband's mother except bring her children into overmuch contact with her. She said: 'We'll have to see, won't we? They are such *busy* little things at the weekends. Now, is there anything we can do for you?'

'Not that I know of,' said Viola ungraciously. 'I'm not a complete cripple yet. In any case, I imagine Hilary will be round tonight. He's always willing to turn his hand to anything.'

Normally Desmond was pleased to hear that his brother was doing his share of what he privately called 'oldie-watching', but tonight he merely said 'Good', with a preoccupied expression on his face, and made for the hall.

At the front door, as she watched them go down the garden path, with their jolly waves and their toothpaste smiles, Viola shouted: 'And if you see that father of yours again, you can tell him it won't do. It won't do at all. Nothing to be gained by our meeting. I wouldn't make him comfortable at all!'

Driving home in the car, Desmond and Margaret had a frank and open discussion on the subject of the books, the money, and brother Hilary. Knowing nothing about the likely sums involved, or the intentions of Viola's younger son, the discussion was inconclusive, but as he stopped his car outside its magnificent, unpaid-for garage, Desmond said: 'I think I'd better keep an eye on young Hilary.'

And Margaret said: 'I'm going to find out what a best-seller might bring in. Just for interest's sake.'

They smiled at each other in perfect understanding.

Later that same evening, Hilda Machin and her daughter were playing Scrabble by the window of Hilda's first-floor sitting-room, when the garden gate into the street opened and admitted a square, ruddy, grinning man of thirty-five or so, swinging in his large hand an unwrapped bottle of something.

'Hilary too,' said Hilda. 'Madam's getting popular in her old age. Or is it the vultures gathering?'

'Hilary's not like that,' said Rose, struggling with a handful of vowels, but watching him from the corner of her eye as he made his way nonchalantly up the path.

Later in the evening the sound of loud laughter wafted up through the open window, and even snatches of a song. The evening visit of Hilary Seymour-Strachey seemed to have taken on a very different character to the afternoon one of his brother and sister-in-law.

'Typical Hilary,' said Rose, listening abstractedly. 'He really is nice.'

Her mother looked up from her letters, and gazed hard at her daughter. Another great gust of delighted laughter came from downstairs.

'Oh yes, there's a lot of Walter in young Hilary,' said Hilda quietly.

By the time her daughter caught the impact of the words, Hilda was intently laying her word out on the board.

CHAPTER V

THE WORLD OF LEARNING

The room on the first floor of Meadowbanks, Viola Machin's house, in which Mr Kronweiser plied his research was very tiny indeed. A gimcrack modern desk table ('Good enough for him') had been placed there, and there were a few shelves, stocked with the works of Walter Machin, cheap editions of Lawrence, Walter Greenwood, Orwell, Sillitoe and others, and copies of periodicals which had contributed to the revival of interest in Machin's books. These were the basic tools of Mr Kronweiser's research, and the study was only just big enough to hold them and him.

Dwight Kronweiser came to this room every day, spending his mornings going through the manuscript fiction, personal letters and other papers which had been stored in the attic for thirty years before his arrival. He made transcripts of the fiction, and of all the other major documents. These he carried home, partly because the little room lacked storage space, partly to appease the secretive, magpie instinct which was part of his nature: he loved to keep, hide, obfuscate, cover his tracks; he had fantasies in the watches of the night of other scholars stealing a march on him and publishing the definitive study of Walter Machin first (though how that would be possible, in view of his privileged position, he would have been hard put to it to say). He saw mainly the cloak and dagger aspects of scholarship, and acted accordingly.

Home, for Mr Kronweiser, was a large bedroom in a working-class house to the north of the town. In spite of his expressed desire to soak up atmosphere, he did not feel at home there. His landlady didn't understand him. So he spent long days and evenings at Meadowbanks, working (when he had done a stint of transcription) on the manuscript which was destined to be the Walter Machin volume in the Payne's Great Authors series of monographs. He sat at his desk, the edge pressed hard against his belly, seeming not to have an ounce of surplus bone in his body, meditating, cogitating, moulding his concrete blocks of critical prose:

> The major problem Machin confronts in *The Factory Whistle* is that of irrelation, which in its turn is his means of defining the absolute. The complementary, interpenetrating phenomena in proletarian life that the implied narrator confronts, and by confronting epiphanizes, are a means primarily of defining his own ambivalent relation both to the zeitgeist and to his own eternal validity.

Mr Kronweiser stared at the ceiling in creative agony for a space, and then, neatly scoring through the word 'validity', he substituted 'authenticity'.

Having changed this stage in the argument to his liking, Dwight Kronweiser began contemplating his next deathless paragraph, and gazed fixedly ahead of him as polysyllabic concepts moved through his mind like heavy artillery on parade. In the middle of this elephantine travail, there came a knock on the door. Mr Kronweiser's reaction was odd: he sprang to a crouch over his manuscript, then put a piece of clean paper over it. Then he blinked his eyes nervously, and said: 'Yes?'

It was Hilda Machin, peeping round the door with
a cocksparrow expression, like the coming of spring.

'Well, hello, Mrs—er—Machin, this is an honour,'
said Dwight Kronweiser, uncurling himself from his
protective position, then getting up with an attempt
at expansiveness. 'I appreciate your looking me up in
my cubby-hole, I really do. Now, do sit down a moment—we can just fit another chair in here.'

And he bustled out on to the landing to fetch a
straight-backed chair that stood there for no particular reason. As he did so, he kept darting his eyes nervously back to his little room and the manuscript on
the desk; but when he got back in, puffing a little, he
was smiling and giving little mutters of pleasure:
'Well, this sure is nice of you, real friendly . . .'

Hilda Machin settled herself down on the chair,
smiling happily and looking guilelessly at Mr Kronweiser who, if the truth were known, amused her very
much. She looked disparagingly round his little
cubby-hole as he squeezed his belly back into its
pouch in the middle of the desk.

'You *are* cramped in here, aren't you?' she said.
'She could have given you a bit more room.'

'Believe me, I'm deeply grateful to be given any
sort of study at all, deeply grateful. Just the chance to
transcribe the manuscripts was *the* most fantastic
luck, the greatest thing that's ever happened to me.
I'd have been happy to transcribe them just any-
place.'

'Oh, we wouldn't want to let them out of our
sight,' said Hilda. Mr Kronweiser was unsure about
that 'we': was it a plural, or was it an ironic reference
to Viola Machin? He laughed nervously. 'Anyway, she
could have given you the study downstairs,' continued
Hilda. 'It's not used, and that way you could have
kept everything together. You've no room here to
keep anything at all.'

'Oh, I keep everything at home—I file them there, on my own system,' said Mr Kronweiser eagerly. 'I shouldn't in any case keep the originals and the transcripts in one place, no sir. You never know what might eventuate.'

'Really?' said Hilda, wide-eyed. 'What sort of eventuations had you in mind? Burglary? Fire?'

'Believe you me, anything can happen,' said Mr Kronweiser, with gloomy relish. 'Friend of mine at Duke—had his Ph.D stolen—all the manuscripts, notes, card indexes, the whole caboodle! It turned up a year later, all rewritten but basically identical, as a Ph.D at San Diego. No kidding! And there wasn't a damned thing he could do about it. Another guy had his in his car. Parked it to buy a pack of cigarettes— the car was stolen by a couple of kids going joy-riding. They used the Ph.D to light a bonfire to barbecue some steaks they'd nicked. Judge said he couldn't put an estimate on the value of the typescript, and ignored it in the sentence. Boy! That guy was sore as a cowboy's . . .' Mr Kronweiser faded out abruptly and subsided into coughs. He was sweating heavily with emotion.

'Ee, well, you do lead exciting lives,' said Hilda Machin. 'I'd never have guessed.'

'Others just buy and sell them,' continued Kronweiser lugubriously. 'Regular black market. Three thous the going rate, or was a few years back. No go nowadays. The bottom's dropped right out of the market.'

'Oh? Why's that?'

'Hell, with eighty per cent of Ph.Ds unemployed, what's the point?'

'So that's why you keep your transcripts at home, is it?' said Hilda, still looking at Kronweiser with an expression of absorbed interest. 'I suppose it is safer.'

'Hell yes. And I mail a carbon to Jackson's. That

way we're triply safe. Anyway, I'm through with the
fiction, so that side of it's sewn up.'

'Really? Is it all transcribed?'

'Yep. Finished the last short story today—baring un-
foreseen discoveries, naturally.'

'Which one is that?' asked Hilda, putting out her
hand towards the manuscript on the desk. Mr Kronweiser sprang into his earlier stance of crouching
flabby tiger, then with a deprecatory smile he relaxed
stiffly and began rummaging in the top drawer.
'That's my manuscript there,' he said hesitantly;
'naturally I feel its manifest imperfections.' He took
out a typescript, to which was attached a handwritten
manuscript. With visible reluctance he handed it to
Hilda Machin.

'Oh, one of the early ones,' she said brightly, han-
dling the work of her late husband with no notable
reverence, and casually flicking through it. 'Handwritten. Yes, I remember it. He wrote it—let's see—one
wet Sunday. It must have been about nineteen thirty-
seven or eight. It's a poor piece, or so he thought. He
didn't include it in *Cotton Town*.'

'Very true. But there were one or two deeply interesting passages in that story, invaluable for the thesis
I shall present in my study of his work. And it will
fill out the new volume of shorter pieces too.'

Hilda, deep in her reading, nevertheless perked up
at this and shot a sharp glance in Mr Kronweiser's
direction. 'Oh, so there will be *two* new volumes, will
there?'

'That's right. The second novel, of course, and
then the shorter pieces—stories and some newspaper
articles, and so on. We should easily make it into two
hundred pages or so.'

'Well, I'm glad about that. What are you going to
call them? I suppose it will be you as will give them
their titles?'

'In the case of the novel that won't be necessary. He left behind a list of alternatives. Perhaps you'd like to have a look at them?'

On Hilda Machin's nodding, Mr Kronweiser calmly took back the copy of the short story and the original manuscript, clipped them together, and put them back carefully in their right place in the drawer. Then he went to another drawer and extracted a piece of paper, squinting at it carefully before he handed it over.

'This is it,' he said. 'Just as he left it.'

The typescript (with odd mis-spellings and typing errors reproduced from the original) ran to nine or ten titles. Hilda Machin read it with every appearance of interest. '*Spinning Jenny*', she said with contempt. 'Pretty obvious that. *The Loom of Age*—now that really would put people off: what was Walter thinking of? *Satanic Mills*—bit overdone: he made a nice enough living out of them. . . . Ee, they're all a bit tired, aren't they?'

'You have no preferences, then?'

'Not I. You might as well call it *Trouble up at t'Mill* and have done with it as far as I'm concerned. You know, I think the thing was that he was out of date, and by the time he wrote the second book he knew it. He began too late. If he'd started in the early 'thirties, when we were courting and when the Depression was really biting, then he'd have done all right. But all Walter thought about at that time was slap and tickle in the grass, and you can quote me on that, as knows. But it was years before he got started, and 'thirty-nine before he got published. By then it was too late. People were tired of that sort of thing. Then there was t'war and all. Poor old Walter. He missed the band-wagon.'

The list dropped from her hand, and Mr Kronweiser seized on it to restore it to its place.

'It's heart-warming,' volunteered Mr Kronweiser, 'that justice will be done to him at last.'

'I don't suppose it will warm *his* heart,' said Hilda.

'So I'll note down that you have no special wishes about the title, then, Mrs Machin.'

'Not really. I haven't read the book, or not much of it, that I remember. I suppose *Tripe and Onions* was the best of them. One of the ones with "tripe" in it, anyway.'

Dwight Kronweiser looked at her hard, blinking his pale, short-sighted eyes. Hilda Machin pulled herself up and looked at her wristwatch in mock consternation.

'Well, this isn't getting the cow milked. What I came for was, I brought that letter you were talking about.'

'The one from London?'

'That's the one. I found it in my old snap album. Daft place to put it, but there . . . He talks about seeing his publisher, and getting a better contract for the next book. It was June, 'thirty-nine, as you can see. I knew I'd *had* a letter from him then, because it was the last time we were apart before he was called up.'

'Hmm, hmm,' said Mr Kronweiser, reading the letter through with little snuffles of academic contentment. 'Neat! Very good. I'm deeply grateful to you, Mrs Machin, deeply grateful. I'll see you get it back in no time at all.'

'Oh, don't worry,' said Hilda, getting up to go. '*I'm* not sentimental about him, you know—far from it.'

'Now you do yourself an injustice there, I know. As I say, I'll get it back to you just as soon as I've managed to make a copy of it.'

'And you'll file it with the other stuff, will you?' asked Hilda Machin at the door. 'Infinite riches in a little room?'

As she closed the door after her, Mr Kronweiser looked at it for a minute or two in puzzlement. Wasn't that some sort of quotation? He couldn't quite place it. Not his period, anyway. Or was it a proverb? Either way, he couldn't make that dame out. What's more, he didn't like her—which meant, in Kronweiser idiom, that he didn't trust her—which meant, in its turn, that she was not wholly devoted to the interests of Dwight Kronweiser, MA, Ph.D. What was she up to? What made her tick? How sharp was she? He didn't like the way her accent changed, he didn't like the way she'd sit there looking cosy as a mother chook and then shoot a sharp glance at him, like she understood him through and through. Mr Kronweiser didn't know where he stood with her, and he hated that feeling.

He looked back to the letter, and went through it again—still thinking and frowning.

That night, as Hilda Machin was boiling milk in the kitchen for her good-night cup of coffee, an unusual thing happened. Viola Machin came to the kitchen. Came quite deliberately, though as usual Hilda had made plenty of noise coming down the stairs to ensure that her presence was known. On Viola's approach down the hall, Hilda turned up the gas and made preparation for a hasty departure, but this, it seemed, was not the idea.

'No, no, don't hurry, Hilda,' said Viola, sailing in, all arrogant bosom and cold cream, but smiling condescendingly. She went to the bread bin and seemed to be preparing to make herself a piece of toast. Hilda did not turn down the gas. 'We have been a little silly sometimes in the past, don't you think, Hilda?' went on Viola. 'I'm sure that once in a while we can be in the same kitchen without explosions occurring, don't you agree? We are civilized people, after all.'

'Aye, 'appen,' said Hilda.

Nothing annoyed Viola Machin more, as a general rule, than Hilda putting on the broad Lancashire. It seemed to her like an assertion of closeness to the dead Walter that she could not match. But tonight her face seemed frozen into its gracious expression, like royalty in a traffic jam, and if she wished to herself that Hilda would make the odd concession so that civil conversation with her could be easier, nothing of this appeared in her manner.

'Mr Kronweiser seems to be getting on very nicely with the transcriptions,' said Viola, slotting the bread into the toaster.

'Oh aye?' said Hilda.

'You went to see him this morning . . . ?'

'That's right.'

Viola Machin repressed a sigh. 'Did you have anything interesting to show him?'

'Well,' said Hilda, raising her voice slightly, 'I didn't go for the pleasure of his company. I didn't go because I was suddenly seized by an overwhelming passion for him, we didn't make love on the tiger-skin rug in that little box of a room you gave him, his pear-shaped body pressed against my ageing but still voluptuous frame.'

Viola Machin left a few moments' pause. You know, I've always thought it was your sense of *humour* that attracted Walter to you, Hilda.'

'Because otherwise it's totally inexplicable, eh?'

'Now, Hilda, let's not start that *silly* bickering, please. You can't say I came here tonight wanting a row—that you *can't* say.'

'No, you came here wanting to know what I'd been saying to Mr Kronweiser today.'

Viola Machin, seated in a dignified pose on the corner of the kitchen table, her white and pale blue

brunch coat billowing around her, found her pose of
aggrieved innocence difficult to keep up.

'All right, all right. I admit it,' she said.

'And the answer is: I took him a letter.'

'Oh yes—er—one of Walter's?'

'One of Walter's,' said Hilda, looking concentrated-
ly at Viola. 'When he was in London. Seeing his
publishers. June nineteen thirty-nine. OK?'

'Was there anything in it? Anything . . . *personal*?'

'He sent his love. Is that all right? Not too hot to
handle, for an old-fashioned family publisher like
Jackson's? Oh, and there was love and kisses for Rose
too.'

'I see. So there was nothing more . . . controver-
sial. Well, I'm glad. I'm sure he'll find it very useful.
I'm looking forward to reading his book.'

'So'm I. Don't get many good laughs these days.'

'Now *Hilda*! I'm sure he'll do a very good job . . .'

'The idea of a chap like *that*, writing a book on
Walter: it's enough to make the cat laugh.'

'Well, he was *interested*—and he was the first. Of
course, if I'd waited just a few months, I could have
had anyone I liked. But there: I couldn't have known
the interest there'd be.'

'There's one comfort,' said Hilda, sipping her
coffee. 'He treats his manuscript like a mummy lion
her cubs. With a bit of luck he won't be able to bear
to part with it to a publisher. Save us all a lot of red
faces.'

'I don't think, Hilda, that you're approaching this
revival of interest in Walter's work in the right frame
of mind.'

'Oh me—I'm tickled pink. If I wasn't, I wouldn't
have kept quiet about you and him, would I?'

Viola Machin, torn between a desire to protest that
she had nothing to hide, and a feeling that she had,

said at last, reluctantly: 'Well, yes, that's true: and I'm grateful to you for that, Hilda.'

'So you should be. But there's one thing, Viola, that I don't think you really realize.'

'What's that?'

'That Kronweiser. You think he's an idiot, because he gets things wrong—the background, the politics, Walter, us. And he does, all the time. But: he's not stupid, Viola. He's not stupid. And I think we both ought to realize that. Otherwise—'

Hilda Machin looked at her husband's second wife, raised an eyebrow, and then flopped in her furry slippers down the hall. Viola Machin bent heavily over the table buttering her toast—very, very thoughtful.

CHAPTER VI

RELATIONSHIPS

Rose Clough, née Machin, lived on the outskirts of Oswaldston on a spick and span, jerry-built private estate. The houses were each slightly different from each other; here a window was larger, there a door had been moved round the corner—no one family's was quite the same as his neighbour's. In spite of which, the impression they gave was of being identical, and it was left to the owners to give their property whatever signs of individuality they could, by making neat little gardens, or by not doing so, by cleaning the windows once a month, or by not doing so. Rose Clough's was one of the not doing so houses.

Rose had married late. She had had a good time in her twenties: a good job as a doctor's receptionist (she had gone against the general rule for the species by being warm and sympathetic, though she stood no more nonsense than was inescapable). She had had plenty of boyfriends, some casual, some of longer duration. Some of them had asked her to marry them, but life had seemed too good to settle down. But then she had been thirty, and then thirty-three, and the panic that overtakes women of that age, even in the nineteen seventies, had come upon her, and the desire to have a child, which she had hardly thought about before. When Bill Clough proposed, she accepted him and came to live at Petworth Estate.

Bill Clough was a small grocer, with a nice little

shop in a working-class area, where he had managed
to survive the competition from the big chains by
being convenient, not outrageously dear, and usually
cheerful. You could always have a bit of fun with
Bill, people said. After marriage he had got fatter,
and less lively. He had married because he too
thought he was of an age to settle down, and he had
settled. He liked big fatty meals, twice a day if possible, and a noisy sleep after them. He loved his little
daughter, but he wished she had less energy. He
watched the television at night, all night, making remarks like 'That's a bit of all right' at the girls, or
'Kill him' to the wrestlers. On Saturday afternoons he
shouted advice to the televised footballers, but often
fell asleep the next minute, with a can of light ale in
his hand.

It was not the marriage Rose would have chosen
for herself, now.

When Jackson's, from courtesy, sent six copies of
the new edition of *The Factory Whistle* to Hilda
Machin, she was round to her daughter's with one
the same day. Rose left it on the coffee table by her
husband's chair, and when he had had his usual
mixed fry-up and was preparing to have his snooze,
his eye caught it as it lay there.

'Oh ah, that's your dad's book, is it?' he said, and
picked it up. Rose realized with a shock that she had
never seen him handle a book before, and watched
him curiously.

'Well I never,' he said, uncertainly.

'It's nicely got up, isn't it?' she said, to help.

'Looks champion to me, not that I'd know,' said
Bill. He lost interest when he found there were no
pictures. 'Now I come to think of it,' he said, easing
himself down into the depths of his very easy chair,
'that Mrs Entwhistle from the corner said there was
something about your dad in one of the Sunday pa-

pers, I don't remember which.' He had an odd air of being impressed, but quite bewildered. 'A whole article, she said.'

'That's right. I should have gone out and bought them, but I forgot. Mum's got them all.'

'Seems funny, after all this time. I can't make head nor tail of it.'

'He's being rediscovered. They're going to do a piece on Mum in the local paper—the reporter's been along already. She's very chuffed it's her and not Viola.'

'Oh aye? That'll make folk talk. Good for business. You'd better tell me all about your dad, so I can keep my end up.' He seemed about to drop off as he said: 'Pity it's Viola who'll be raking in the dough, isn't it?'

'Oh, I don't know about that,' said Rose. An eye opened, enquiringly. 'She owns the copyright, but Mum owns the manuscripts. Dad left them to her when he died.'

'I didn't know that,' said Bill Clough, fighting sleep.

'That's really how they came to team up as they did, and live in the same house. The stuff had just stayed there for years, and Mum hadn't been interested, but then people started talking about Dad, and writing to her, and sending pieces they'd written on him. Then when her house was due for demolition, she and Viola met, and Viola asked what should be done with the manuscripts, as she was thinking of selling the house. It was too big for her when the boys left home, and she couldn't really afford it any more. So they decided to split the house in two.'

'I don't see the use of a lot of old papers, though. You can't make anything out of them.'

'There's a lot of unpublished manuscripts—one of them's Dad's second novel. They'll be coming out

over the next year or so. I think Mum's come to some
sort of agreement with Viola over the profits. She'll
be getting her share. Do you know, they say Dad
might become some sort of classic?'

'Never,' said Bill.

'So Mum says. She thought it was a huge joke. You
know her. But if so, there'll be money coming in.
And it'll go on, too—a real little nest egg.'

Bill Clough lay thinking about this for some time.
'Well, I don't know owt about that sort of thing, but
it seems rum to me,' he said. 'Let's just hope so, eh,
Rosie? Because it'll come to you, won't it? I mean,
there's no one else in the family, is there? It'll be
yours when she goes.'

'Oh yes,' said Rose, 'it'll be mine.'

Later that evening Rose Clough, walking her dog,
met Hilary Seymour-Strachey, walking his dog. This
happened rather often, and if the inhabitants of
Oswaldston had not mostly been shut up in front of
their televisions at this time of day, it might already
have given rise to some talk. Anyone seeing them together on the common outside Oswaldston would
have taken them for husband and wife, though Hilary was by nearly three years the younger. He was
stocky, gay (in the antiquarian use of the word) and
nut-brown-haired, with a great sense of daring and
mischief. He was a freelance commercial artist, and a
painter of potential but too little application. Rose,
fairer, with a good slim figure and a large share of
her mother's charm, had the same confidence and
pleasure in life. They made a good, pair, people
would have said who saw them. Rose had often
thought the same. Tonight, though, she kept her distance.

'What's up, Rosie?' asked Hilary, watching their
spaniel and labrador rolling over the twilit green
turf. 'It's not like you to be so chilly. What's up?

"The Awakened Conscience" by Holman Hunt stuff, is that it? I never liked that picture. Have the Methodies been getting at you?'

'The Methodists never made much headway with the Machin family,' said Rose, still keeping her distance and not looking him in the eye. 'Perhaps it would have been better if they had.'

'There, I knew it. Thoughts of hell flames are blighting your young life. Anticipations of being skewered on a fork and toasted for indulgence in the sins of the flesh. Or is it just that your old man's found us out?'

'Not him. I'd have to play him home movies of us in bed before he'd twig.'

'I've never met your old man. I don't somehow think we'd have much in common.'

'You wouldn't. No reason why I should jump from the frying-pan into the frying-pan, is there?'

'There you see—fire and burning at the back of your mind again. What gives, Rosie?'

Rose Clough whistled the dogs to order. They stopped rollicking for a couple of seconds and looked impertinently in their direction. Then they went at it with redoubled glee. Rose walked on thoughtfully for a bit, then she turned to Hilary and said: 'You went to see your mother last week, didn't you?'

'That's right. Had a fine old time. This Machin revival's putting new life into her. I think I'll paint her one of these days: "The Triumphant Widow"; "Confidence Justified"—something like that. She's like a cat that's found a way to milk cows.'

'I was round at Mother's that night.'

'That's right. Mother said so: "That Rose is round again tonight." Sniff.'

'Did she say anything more about me?'

'Well, if you want to know, she said: "Of course,

she's quite pre*sent*able, but I always think there's just the tiniest bit of the tart there." '

'Old bitch.'

'True. But an *interesting* old bitch.'

'And what did you say in reply?'

'I think I said "That's how I like them"—and got a filthy look for my pains.'

'She didn't say anything else?'

'No. What is all this, then, Rose? Why the hell should you worry what my mother says about you, for God's sake. It's no skin off your nose, is it? I've never noticed you or your mum pay that much attention to old Vi's opinions up to now.'

'Do you think she knows about us?'

'I'm damned sure she doesn't. Nobody knows about us. Yet.'

'What do you think she'd say?'

'Something snooty, I'd bet. Come off it, Rosie, spill the beans. What is this all about?'

'Something Mum said . . . We were listening to you both downstairs, and we heard you laugh . . . like you do . . . and Mum said: "There's a lot of Walter in Hilary."'

There was a moment's silence while Hilary Seymour-Strachey digested this. Then he burst out into his great chortling laugh. 'The old devil! I knew your mum was a wag. What was she doing? Warning you off me?'

'I don't know *what* she was doing.'

'She'd probably heard rumours, and didn't like you fraternizing with the enemy camp.'

'You just said that nobody suspected.'

'OK, then you gave the game away yourself. I love you like—' he was going to say 'like a sister', but he suddenly changed his mind—'I love you to distraction, Rosie, but I can read your mind like a book, and I expect your mum can too. She's a sharp old bird. You talked about me, old Hilda saw the love-light gleaming, and she warned you off. In a thoroughly sneaky, underhand way, I may say, but there it is. I bet that's how it was.'

'My Mum's not sneaky—'

'Don't you believe it. People get like that when they get older. Look at my mother. She used to be—well— blatant is the only word for it. But she's got sneakier and sneakier as she's got more and more respectable. Don't let your mother's down-to-earth Lancashire Lassie airs fool you. She switches them on and off like the electric light.'

'You hardly know Mum.'

'Well enough. Come off it, Rosie. Don't let it worry you. It's just the oldies trying to put a spoke in our wheel. I don't even think old Vi knew your dad before I was born.'

'Yes, she did. You were born in nineteen-forty. They all knew each other well before the war—all four of them.'

'Well, I do know Gerald didn't disappear out of our lives until 'forty-three, because Des told me so. The whole thing split apart when he went to Grimsby.'

'That doesn't prove anything,' said Rose. 'Especially if your mother was as you say.'

'What do you mean?'

'Blatant.'

They walked on in silence for a time, and then Hilary said: 'I still think you mum's playing a dirty game, or she's imagining things. I expect everything that went on then's churning round in her mind because of this new wave of interest in those awful books.'

'Didn't you like them?'

'I only read the first one. I thought it was pretty synthetic. But the point is all the old grudges churn round in her mind, and she looks at me and fancies all sorts of things. But the fact is, she can't possibly *know*.'

'True,' admitted Rose. Then she nastily added: 'Perhaps even Viola doesn't.'

'I never made her out to be the Lady of the Camellias,' protested Hilary. As they neared houses, and the beginnings of Oswaldston with its twilit grime, he said: 'Anyway, even if it were true, would it worry you, Rosie?'

Rose laughed and looked more happy. 'No, I dare say it wouldn't, after a time,' she said.

But they soon separated, and took different ways home.

CHAPTER VII

HIGH WORDS

On Friday, 4 May Viola Machin spent most of the day answering correspondence. In the last week it had positively snowed letters and business. *The Factory Whistle* had been republished a few days before, and beside her Viola kept the pile of six copies sent her by the publishers, with its Lowry-ish cover of tall chimneys and matchstick men. The Sunday newspaper articles had come out the week before last, and were still bringing in letters. Some of these were begging letters from old mill-workers in financial distress, and these Viola consigned to the wastepaper basket, whether or not the writers claimed nebulous acquaintanceship with her late husband. Others wrote about what Walter Machin's books had meant to them at the time of their publication, and to these Viola wrote faintly magisterial replies of thanks and interest which usually also contained subtle plugs for the two books which were as yet unpublished. Other people wrote with personal memories of the author, and these were divided up: some were handed over to Mr Kronweiser, as keeper of the Machin Archive; some were retained by Viola; and some went the way of the begging letters. All received replies, of varying degrees of warmth.

The letter which concluded the day for Viola Machin was not one of the ones that pleased her most. It read:

* * *

I was one of Walter Machin's classmates at Burnley Road Primary School, and I was very interested to read the interesting article in the *Sentinel* and look at the interesting pictures. I am the little boy to the left of the picture of his class half hidden by the boy next to me how funny to think of Walter being an author as he was always in trouble at school and none of the teachers could make him learn doesn't it make you think. But he was always having fun so I suppose its the imagination that counts isn't it. Hoping this finds you as it leaves me we are none of us getting any younger Yours Sincerely Fred Bottomley.

To this Viola wrote a reply expressing lukewarm interest. With difficulty she repressed comments on the writer's own linguistic proficiency, and how in her view it disabled him from judging Walter's scholastic achievements; with difficulty, too, she refrained from rebutting the idea that she was not getting any younger, for that was precisely what she felt she was getting, these days; and she ended with best wishes for the future, mentally hoping it would not be for him a long one. Then she consigned the letter to the wastepaper basket.

Her labours done—and though they involved both effort and expense she enjoyed them very much—she sat for a little at her desk, thoughtful and handsome. She was wearing the dark green woollen dress that showed off her still remarkable contours. Then she got up, rather stiffly, and busied herself making tea and thin bread and butter, an invariable meal, but always a treat. After it she felt soothed of any irritation she may have felt with the last letter, wiped her mouth with satisfaction, and picked up the *Oswald-ston Gazette*.

It was the isssue with the interview with Hilda Machin in. If she had thought of it, she would have looked before; she had registered the reporter and photographer going up to the flat above, and had said to herself that they didn't, very obviously, have the *class* of the young men from the London Sundays. But for some time after she had sat wondering, with a slight undertow of apprehension, what sort of things Hilda would be saying. Because, really, you never knew with Hilda. Now, pursing her lips, she settled down to read.

Her first impressions were very favourable. Even the photograph, she had to admit, was a good one: Hilda would never look attractive, Viola thought to herself, but at least she looked dignified, which was all to the good. Don't want people to think Walter went for the tartish type. The interview opened with reminiscences of their meeting and courtship Suitably bowdlerized, said Viola to herself with a grim smile: if *she* knew Walter, there was a good deal of slap and tickle involved which didn't get into the account. Very sensible of Hilda: nothing is more ridiculous than an old-age pensioner gabbling on about his or her risqué past.

The article went on with an account of Walter and Hilda's early married life, against a background of dole and depression. What kind of a person was Walter Machin then, the interviewer asked?

'Well, he was a charmer,' said Hilda. 'A bobby-dazzler. Ask anyone who knew him. Everyone felt more alive when he was around: there'd be so much fun and games and nonsense—and there was always a bit for everyone, do you know what I mean? He was like a drop of the hard stuff, just when you needed it most.'

Viola relaxed into a mellow mood. Hilda had clearly done her stuff very well. She looked again at the picture: really, Hilda was quite a *pretty* woman in her way, if your tastes inclined you to that sort of good looks. She read on to the story of holidays at Blackpool and Filey, a trip to London, and the gradually expanding horizons which writing brought to Walter. What had made him take up writing in the first place? the interviewer asked.

'Having something to say, I suppose,' said Hilda. 'Unlike some, who think that up afterwards. Anybody who lived through that time in Oswaldston will have a lot of memories of it—some of them bitter, some of them funny. Well, Walter had been through the same things, but he wanted to put them down on paper. I suppose he just felt people ought to know what things were like—people down South, you know. So he wrote them down.'

Quite good, Hilda, thought Viola. Though you do make it sound like running up a cotton frock. Still, she couldn't deny that Hilda had behaved. That warning had had its effect—what a good idea it had been. She must remember to give Greg Hocking a copy of *The Factory Whistle*, suitably inscribed. Viola was beaming benevolently as she read on into the last column. The reporter, treading delicately, had asked if it was a great sorrow to her when she and Walter separated.

'A great sorrow? Ee, I'm not cut out to be a tragedy queen,' said Hilda. That was the tone to take, thought Viola. 'There wasn't owt to be done about it was there? Marriages get broken up every day.'

The writer concluded by—But suddenly Viola pulled herself up in her reading, and went back. Had her concentrated reading of those letters all afternoon made her unduly pernickety? 'Marriages get broken up every day.' No. There it was. Not 'Marriages

break up.' 'Marriages *get broken* up.' A scarlet flush
showed angrily through Viola's powdered cheek. The
bitch, she thought. The low-down bitch. She had to
get her say in, didn't she? Pretending to be so butter-
wouldn't-melt, and then to slide this in—the sharp
kick on the ankle in passing. Did she think I
wouldn't notice? thought Viola, beginning to breathe
heavily. She must think I'm senile if she thought that.
So all Oswaldston will read that, and they'll read between the lines and they'll start calling me the mar-
riage-breaker, will they? And Hilda will be the poor
little wifey at home who had her husband snatched
from her. The sneaky little tart. The two-timing
bitch. The jumped-up mill-girl. I'll show her. I'll get
even with her.

Puffing, Viola struggled to her feet. Clutching her
stick as if it were an offensive weapon, she made for
the door. Her colour had got still more livid and
threatening, and through the fat, purple cheeks her
eyes were bulging and blazing. Those stairs. She
hated those stairs. But it was worth it, to give Hilda
Machin a piece of her mind. It suddenly struck Viola,
in the midst of her rage, that she hadn't had a good
row for months. Nothing like making up for lost
time, she thought to herself with relish.

'All right,' said Hilda Machin, her voice rising. 'I
can't remember whether I did say it or not, but what
if I did? It's the truth, isn't it?'

'It is decidedly not the truth,' boomed Viola. Under
the dark green wool, her breasts were heaving like
pistons. She saw that Hilda's hands were on her hips,
and she knew from experience that this was a danger
signal, but she went on, unintimidated. 'Your marriage broke down. You couldn't hold him, and I don't
wonder, because you had nothing a man like Walter
would want. Then he married me.'

'Oh really? Well, how come he was still married to me when he was demobbed in 'forty-six?'

'He had no intention whatever of going back to you. We had it all arranged.'

'*You* had it all arranged. He had no choice, poor bugger. There was you, waiting at the gates, welcome written all over your tits and panting for him. He was weak as ditch-water, and he went along.'

Viola's voice began to boom, like an English contralto slaughtering Handel. 'He told me a fortnight before he came out that he'd be coming to me.'

'Oh really? By letter? I'd love to see *that* example of his Collected Works!'

'By phone, of course.'

'Naturally. But no doubt you went along just in case. While we sat round at home in little old Oswaldston, waiting for Daddy to come back. And all we got was a lousy phone call three weeks later. Made while you had one of his arms in a half-Nelson behind his back, I'd guess, or a gun in his ribs. "I'm not coming back, Hilda, gulp, gulp." My God, I thought my Walter had a bit more gumption. I knew then you'd done for him all right.'

'Done for him? I'd have made him, if he'd lived. He was too good for you, Hilda Machin, and that's what you hadn't got the brains to understand. You were nothing to him by then, nothing. He needed a real woman, not a shrew from the gutter.'

'And is that what he got?' While Viola tended to boom under stress, Hilda's voice became higher and more satirical. 'Go on with you. Walter was like a squeezed-out rag after he married you. He wasn't even good at his job. Ask anybody round here. They'd hardly believe it was the same man.'

'What does that prove? Plenty of men couldn't settle back into the old ruts after the war. I'd have thought less of Walter if he could. He was too good

for this place. I was mad to let him bring me here.
He could have done anything—anything.'

'What had you in mind? Not the writing, was it?
Would you have made him into the working-class
Christopher Fry? Don't make me laugh. He went
back to the mill because he knew he belonged there.
It was the only place he could go. But you'd got hold
of him, and you'd squeezed him till the pips rattled,
and you'd done for him as a man. Like you did Gerald—'

'LEAVE GERALD OUT OF THIS!'

'—until he got away. Slipped out from under your
sweaty embrace. Lucky old Gerald. I always did ad-
mire him, in a way. He did it just in time. He's still
alive, I hear.'

'Still alive, and wanting to marry me again—as if
I'd give him the chance!'

'Go on, he never is? Well, I've heard of old lags
wanting to die in jail, so I suppose it figures. Why
don't you take up the offer? It would be very fitting:
you could both live off the royalties, and go out with
a bang.'

'I have no intention of "going out" yet awhile,
Hilda Machin. I'll live to see you underground, I can
tell you that. I must say I'm seeing a new side to you
today, and I ought to have suspected it before. Walter
always did say you were underhand.'

'Did he now? Well, you should have heard what he
said about you, first time we met. I remember him.
We were in a shabby little hole in Paddington, and
when we came back from the pub that night he went
walking up and down that hotel room, sticking his
chest out and saying, 'I'm the sex queen of
Bloomsbury. Come and get me while I'm still hot!"
Ee, I can see him now. He always was a wonderful
mimic, was our Walter.'

'Oh yes? And did he tell you we made love the next

night? Ah—that got you. He didn't, I can see. "You were looking after Rose. We sent Gerald out to the local to get a bottle of Scotch. We knew he'd have a quick one while he was there. We arranged it all just by looking at each other.'

'Aye,' said Hilda quietly. 'He did have talking eyes.'

'So I don't think he found me *quite* so ridiculous as you make out,' concluded Viola, with an angry smirk of triumph.

'Oh, he didn't mind them ridiculous,' said Hilda, perking up again. 'Big or small, fat or thin, sensible or silly, it didn't worry Walter. If he hopped into bed with you that night, he was only doing what he'd done with a hundred and one others.'

'I'm glad you admit it. So you can hardly say I broke your marriage up, can you?'

'Oh, that was different. The others were just a thing of the moment. A quick in and out after the pubs closed or round the back of the factory. I expect that's what he thought he was going to when you grabbed him at the end of the war. He should have realized it would be different with Gerald gone. You wanted a man, and you wanted him for good—because after all, you were getting on then, weren't you? So once you got him into your fleshy arms—'

'My arms were not fleshy!'

'—well, they surely are now—and you hugged him tighter and tighter, and you dragged him through the divorce courts—'

'You co-operated willingly enough!'

'I'd too much pride to do anything else. And then you dragged him to the altar, or was it the registrar?—I've never had an account of the joyful occasion—and then you came back up here, and you thought you'd be Queen of Oswaldston, with your little private income, and your nice stone house, and your upper-class ways.'

'He dragged me up here. What was I supposed to do in a common little hole like this?'

'And when you got back here, everyone could see that Walter was just a shell, just a husk you'd had all the goodness out of. He wasn't even up to being works foreman any longer, quite apart from anything else. They'd have sacked him, if it hadn't been for his war-record—it wouldn't have looked good. And that was the end of Walter Machin. You sucked him dry.'

'I did not suck him dry! He was sick!'

'Yes. I reckon he was glad to die when he did. There wasn't much left for him, was there?'

'What do you mean, wasn't much left? He was happy! He loved me! He loved the children!'

'Oh yes, he probably did love the children. People like Walter always do get on well with children.'

'What do you mean?'

'People who are soft and good-humoured. He spoilt Rose that much he'd have ruined her if I'd let him. The trouble with Walter was, he could never say no to anyone. As you found out very quickly. But I'm glad he had the boys, I really am. Because there wasn't much love in the house otherwise, from what I hear.'

'Oh, you hear what you want to hear.'

'Folk say you nagged him to death, Viola.'

Viola Machin's face, still an unhealthy vivid red, twisted itself into an expression of contempt. 'And how do these "folk" know, eh? Don't make me laugh. It's not as though the house was full of servants, listening at the doors. My income and his pay packet didn't run to that.'

'Oh, folk knew because Walter told them. All the factory. You probably didn't realize about Walter: he never could keep anything back—a right old woman like that, he was.'

'If people told you he said that, it was to make you

feel better. We had a wonderful marriage—it was full, it was funny, it was loving—it was everything a marriage should be. He'd never known what it could be like before. How could he with you? You may have been his class, but you were too limited for a man like him.'

'Limited, eh? Is it "Walter, the great intellectual" now, eh?'

'He had more brains in his little finger than you have in your whole skinny body.'

'If he was that smart, Viola, he would never have fallen for your little game. Because he had your number. Even Walter could tell you were a ninety-ninth-rate poetess with a grand manner, and a liking for getting people in your coils. He'd got your number the first time we met. So it was really stupid of him to let you catch him after all. That's what I can't forgive—that he should be so gormless!'

Viola, pretending to ignore her, took up a theatrical position, as if rapt in the memory of things past: 'Walter was a lovely man. The most marvellous man I ever had in my life. He loved me, and I loved him—we were everything to each other, those brief years we had.' Her back stiffened, and she turned on Hilda: 'People are going to realize that before I've finished.'

'Well, I always knew you'd get your side of the story across loud and clear, Viola. That was never in doubt. So it's mean of you to begrudge me half a sentence.'

'Ah! So it *was* deliberate! I knew it. If I didn't think you'd go blabbing your side of the story all over town, I'd have you out of my house in two shakes.'

'How do you know I won't go? It's no fun living with someone who thinks she's a cross between Virginia Woolf and the Queen Mother. There's nothing to keep me here now, you know. I can afford a place of my own, with the royalties that will be coming in.'

'Who says you'll get anything? It's only a verbal agreement. I'll deny all knowledge of it, if it suits me.'

'Now *that*, Viola, might be very unwise. . . .'

'Now listen to me, Hilda. I've had more than enough of your little games, of your hintings and half-truths and double meanings. You can drive me too far. If you do, I'll forget every agreement we ever had, and I'll fight you with everything I've got, so that by the end you won't have a shred of reputation left—'

'Reputation! That's rich! There are other reputations than mine at risk, you know.'

'I'll see people know the truth about you—'

'The truth, Viola, would be a very dangerous thing to start telling, don't you think?'

Viola Machin, panting, looked hard at Hilda's pert little face looking up at her with a twisted, triumphant smile. Her breath was coming now in sharp, ugly pantings.

'Before I let you foul Walter's memory,' she said, with difficulty, 'I'll drag you through the courts. I'll pull you down into the gutter.' She pulled open the door. 'I'll see you in hell!' she yelled.

The bang of the door resounded all over the house.

CHAPTER VIII

COMBUSTION

The row between the two widows Machin took place between six and six-thirty. It did not remain long unknown. Viola's voice had that organ note of the English landed aristocracy, though in her case it had been formed not in the hunting-fields, but on the lonely, sheep expanses of her native land. It certainly carried in Oswaldston. There was a goodly stretch of garden between Hilda's sitting-room and the road, but later that evening at least three people who had passed by on the other side of the wall commented on the row in the Spinners' Arms.

'By gum, they were going at it,' concluded one, with an appreciative snicker. Lancashire men like women with a bit of fight in them, especially when they direct it at each other.

So that when Greg Hocking, after an evening marking essays, came in at nine-fifteen for a good-night pint, his friend the landlord said: 'Your old girls have been at it today.'

'What do you mean "at it"?' asked Greg apprehensively as if he feared to hear tales of geriatric sex-orgies.

''Ammer and tongs. Arguing. Screaming at each other. There's three or four as 'eard them.'

Greg groaned into his pint mug. Just what he'd hoped to avoid. There was no particular reason why he should have acted as honest broker in this affair, but he had taken it on, and had been quite pleased with himself when he seemed to have brought things off. So far things had apparently gone very smoothly. The articles in the Sunday papers had been well done in their way; the spread of photographs in the *Grub* had made the point Hilda had wanted made without undue underlining; all the local bookshops (two) had piles of copies of *The Factory Whistle* that seemed to diminish rapidly and be renewed. Even the article in the local paper had seemed on a quick glance through earlier to be all right. There had just been that one phrase. . . .

Greg thought to himself: that must have been it. That must have done it.

'Perhaps I'd better go along and see them,' he said. 'See if there's been any harm done.'

'What's the point?' said the landlord, who for some reason had come in the last few weeks to regard the Mrs Machins as in an obscure way a rival show to himself. 'You're not their bloody nursemaid. Why should you go clucking around them like a mother hen, just because they both hit the ceiling?'

He's getting above himself, thought Greg. But he stayed put by the bar.

The news of the noisy row in the big house at the top of the street titillated spasmodic interest in the Spinners' Saloon Bar all evening. Especially as this new bit of gossip came at a time when the idea that Walter Machin was becoming posthumously a national figure was beginning to filter through to Oswaldston consciousness.

'Well, I'll say this,' said one elderly notable: 'We didn't think owt to that Machin when he were alive, and I doubt we'll change our minds thirty years after he's gone.'

It seemed to be the voice of Nottingham, obstinately unimpressed by the national fame of Lawrence.

'I think it'll be a fine thing for the town,' said a
dogmatic little schoolmaster, looking to Greg for ap-
proval in a way he found irritating. 'Put us on the
map. Make people down South realize there's more to
the North than muck and football hooligans. Not
that I've any time for that widow of his. Puts on airs
as if she were running a literary *salon.*'

Alf Ackroyd behind the bar pricked up his ears, as
if some rival establishment to his own were under discussion. There seemed, though, a general lack of enthusiasm for the second Mrs Machin.

'She's basking in all the glory,' said one man, 'but it
had bugger all to do with her. Only married him just
before he died, that I *do* mind. She's a foreigner and
all. Nowt to do with Oswaldston in her life before he
brought her here.'

'I don't think I'd call New Zealanders foreigners,'
ventured Greg Hocking, in protest.

'Well, if they're not that, what are they?' said the
man, obviously finding himself unanswerable.

If the bar conversation was anything to go by, the
people of Oswaldston were going to react to their
newly famous son by first denigrating him and then
resenting any outsider who made claim to him. It
was, Greg Hocking thought, both depressing and
familiar.

But as he was finishing his second pint, and wondering again whether to go up and see one or other
of the Mrs Machins, his mind was made up for him.
First, flashing through the gathering dark, a fire-engine screamed past the window of the Spinners'.
Then a regular popped his head around the door,
like an extra in an old Gracie Fields film, and said:
'Hey, I think there's a fire up at Meadowbanks.'

Dashing his pint mug down on the bar, Greg Hocking darted through the door before any of the idly
curious could bar his way. One glance was sufficient

to show that the regular had been right. From the upstairs window of the grey-stone, substantial house at
the top of the road there was billowing into the night
slow, steady streams of smoke—not thick, or threatening in themselves, but culminating in a heavy, acrid
cloud haloing the house, and sending a hideous smell
of ruin down the gentle hill to the centre of the town.
As Greg broke into a sprint, he saw—almost simulta-
neously—water beginning to play on the upstairs windows, a sudden spurt of flame, and a part of the roof
begin to sag ominously.

Night had closed in. When Greg came to a halt
outside Meadowbanks the scene was lurid, gloomy,
terrifying. The firemen were having trouble with
their hoses on some sides of the house, not being able
to get them close enough to the burning floor to be
effective. At the front, though, they had taken them
through the gate and were playing them on the windows of Hilda Machin's sitting-room. Around the gate
and the two fire-engines parked by it a little knot of
spectators was gathering, increasing by the minute,
kept at a distance by two superbly imperturbable
members of the Lancashire County force. Greg el-
bowed his way through and got behind the engines,
from where he could see into the garden.

'I'm a friend of the old ladies,' he said. 'I want to
go in.'

'You're not allowed,' shouted one of the constables.
'There's no point. We just heard—they've got the old
lady out. She'll be coming any moment. Don't waste
your time.'

Greg looked through the gate. Half-way along the
path, surrounded by shouting, running firemen, was a
little, dark group, moving slowly towards the road.

'*Which* old lady?' Greg shouted to the constable.

'Her as lives here, likely. Is there more than one?'

At that moment both constables' attention was distracted by a little boy who was overcome with curiosity about the working of a fire-engine. Greg dashed through the gate, dodging snaky, shifting hoses on the crazy pavement of the path, and ran towards the slowly moving little group.

It was Viola, helped along by a policeman and a fireman, weeping uncontrollably, her old legs hardly able to bear her, even with support on either side. She was still wearing the green woollen dress, but now her fine figure looked what it was—a wreck of ancient splendour, collapsed, ravaged. Her face, too, bleary, smoky, with deep channels of tears through the make-up, looked like an old woman's—some monster from Restoration comedy, an old, peeling wall. Her voice was so choked with tears and hysteria that, even bending close, Greg could hardly make out her words.

'I was asleep. I dozed off in front of the television. I didn't hear anything. I didn't smell anything. . . . Save my house. Don't let it burn away to nothing. I don't want to go and live with Desmond. . . .' As her voice died away into a mumble, Greg could see from her face that a thought had struck her. She started up with an access of energy. 'Where's Pimpernel? Is he still in there? Save my dog. You can't let him burn.'

'He's outside, lass,' said the fireman soothingly. 'He ran out when we came in to get you.'

'Where's Hilda?' asked Greg urgently. 'Was she in?'

Viola looked at him, sniffing back sobs. 'I don't know. She may have gone to her daughter's. She may have done. I was asleep. I wouldn't have heard.' Then, after a pause, she broke into a howl. 'See that Hilda's all right, Greg. She might be in there. She was my friend—she was! I wouldn't want her to die. Please save her!'

Even as Greg turned to run towards the house, he

seemed to register that Viola's concern for Hilda was
less genuine than her concern for Pimpernel.

The upper storey of Meadowbanks was now belch-
ing thick, angry, black smoke—foul, choking, deso-
late, but Greg had the impression from the activities
of the firemen that the fire was being brought under
control. He ran up to the man that he recognized
through the thick night as the Chief Fire Officer.

'I want to go in,' he said. 'I think there may be
someone still in there.'

'Not a hope,' said the man, hardly looking at him.
'Keep back. We've got the edge on it now. We'll be
sending one of our own men in in a few minutes.'

'It might be too late,' shouted Greg, coughing even
here as he inhaled. 'She's on the first floor.'

'I doubt it,' said the Fire Officer. 'She couldn't have
slept through this. We'd have seen her at the window
long ago, and got her down.'

'If I could just go in—'

'You'll get back and keep out of my way, that's
what you'll do,' said the man, by now justifiably irritated. For the first time he looked Greg in the eye and
pointed towards the gate.

Greg retreated a short way down the path, and the
Fire Officer turned back to the operation. For a moment a breeze cleared the clogging smoke from the
air, and Greg saw, down the path, Viola Machin,
sunk to the ground, sobbing with joy over Pimpernel,
who was prancing agitatedly around her, whining
and barking and twitching his nostrils in sensitive dis-
taste. 'Darling,' she was crooning, 'love. Don't be
frightened, my precious . . .'

Pushing his way through the bushes along the side
of the path, Greg took off into the gardens of
Meadowbanks, flanking the fire-fighting operation
along the front of the house. He kept his eyes fixed
on the upper storey, but there was no sign of life, nor

could he detect any female voice crying through the shouts of the firemen. He skirted down the side of the house, where there were few windows and only one fireman operating, and came to the back. Here everything was in full swing, and he got the impression that the fire was now well under control. He was just meditating whether he could risk running straight in through the kitchen door when he saw two of the firemen in masks, doing just that. A great pillow of smoke billowed out after them. Greg ran up to one of the firemen who was playing his hose on Mr Kronweiser's little room at the back.

'Let me go in with them,' he shouted. 'I know the house. I could direct them.'

'You'd choke to death in half a minute,' said the fireman. 'Keep back. They'll find anyone, if there *is* anyone there.'

'Couldn't I get a mask?'

'Stop inter-bloody-fering. We know our job. Look, if you must do something you can stand at the kitchen door and shout. Tell 'em where the bedroom doors are. I doubt they'll hear, but you never know. But don't take one step inside, I'm warning you.'

The kitchen door was still open, and inside the smoke was clearing. Across the kitchen Greg could see the hallway, but no farther; for there the smoke was trapped. With a sense of futility, he opened his lungs and shouted.

'Go to the bedroom upstairs. It's at the back. Double back at the top of the stairs, and it's the door on the right.'

He listened. There seemed to come a grunt from somewhere. Upstairs, he thought. So they had gone up. He shouted again: 'It's at the back. The back.'

Again he listened. Through the sound of water, and firemen, he thought he heard something again. A shout. A bump. Then at the end of the hall, he saw a shape. A fireman. He had come down the stairs, and was turning towards the kitchen.

'Did you get to the—' But he stopped in the middle of his question. The fireman had something over his shoulder.

Running now, the shape came through the kitchen and out into the garden. The line of fire-fighters opened for him, and he dashed through and out to an open patch of ground. Then he put down his burden. As Greg reached him he was stripping off his mask, and the two of them knelt over the form, laid face upwards on the earth.

It was Hilda Machin, and there was no sign of life.

CHAPTER IX

POST MORTEM

Greg's only real contact at Police Headquarters in Oswaldston was Superintendent Warleigh—met in connection with a case involving one of Greg's students at the College of Further Education, a boy who had been viciously treated throughout his childhood, and was now intent on passing on that treatment to all comers at football grounds up and down the country. Since then they had come into contact over one or two smaller matters, and it was to him that Greg naturally went in the aftermath of Hilda Machin's death.

Superintendent Warleigh was not far off retirement age. He was a kindly man, slow, and far from lively by disposition. He had seen the whole pattern of crime change in the Oswaldston area in the course of his career: crimes that grew out of hunger and desperation had given way to crimes that grew out of affluence, greed, imitation and boredom. None of the changes had given him any added zest for life—or, for that matter, any desire to look for trouble where no trouble was self-evidently present. His remedy for uncertainty was to stroke his moustache, with hard, strong fingers, as if trying to push it back into his upper lip.

'Oh, it's clear enough what happened,' he said to Greg, the day after the fire, standing in the outer office of the Oswaldston station. 'She smelt something, went out of her room, there was smoke on the landing, she went back and got her handbag, ran to the stairs—and then she must have slipped and hit her head. Poor old thing—but she'd had a good life by all accounts.'

'What sort of wound was it on her head?' asked Greg. He was tired and upset, and troubled by a feeling that things did not add up—though without being able to pin down his dissatisfaction.

'A long one, not very deep. May have hit the stair-rail.'

'*Could* she have hurt herself that bad, just by falling?'

'Oh yes, so the doctor says. She came a cropper, no doubt about that, but she was in a hurry, naturally. Oh no—the doctor doesn't have any doubts.'

'I suppose you'll be examining the upstairs—to find out what she fell on to?'

'Have you see the upstairs, lad? Most of the woodwork on the landing and the top of the stairs is charred—some of it burnt to nothing. Of course, we can have a look, but I doubt we'll find anything. In any case, it's not vital. I don't suppose the coroner will make any problems about what happened.'

'And the lungs?'

'Well, according to the doctor she probably died before the fire really got a hold up there. But that figures. She would have smelt it first—long before the old girl downstairs: *she* didn't smell it till we went in to get her.'

'Somehow,' said Greg, going cautiously because he hated to look as if he wanted to teach the police their business, 'it doesn't sound like Hilda Machin. She was very nimble on her pins.'

Superintendent Warleigh spread out his arms in a gesture of hopelessness. 'Old people. You know how it is. Things go wrong, suddenly. I feel it myself, frankly. Suddenly a part of you you've taken for granted all your life gives out, or plays you up. And she panicked, you know. Must have done.'

Greg tried to picture Hilda in her last moments: somehow he failed. He could not associate her with panic. She was too confident, too ironic, too (in an odd way) devil-may-care. She wouldn't have been afraid of death. Though she wouldn't have helped it on its way either. He said: 'What was in the hand-bag?'

'Nothing much. Personal things. Make-up, a bit of money, an old letter. I expect she grabbed it automatically. Women usually do, you know—specially women of that age.'

'Where do you think the fire started.'

'Oh, they say the attic, without a doubt. I gather it was full of old papers and stuff.'

'That must have been the manuscripts. Walter Machin's papers. He was a writer.'

'Aye, I know, lad. I read my papers.'

'Sorry. It's a good job they'd got the second book off to the publishers. It would have been terrible if that had been destroyed. Kronweiser would have gone up the wall.'

'Is that the little Yank? Looks like an Easter egg, and talks like an Act of Parliament?'

'That's him. Has he been around?'

'Yes, this morning. Tut-tutting all round the house. Kept saying: "Thank God I took copies." Boring little creep. He got in everybody's way. I had to send him away.'

'Had he been up in the attic? The papers are his business—not that he'd have wanted to start a fire.'

'The fire was an accident, for Christ's sake. Anyway, he says he went home hours before. I expect one of the old ladies was up there and dropped a fag end or something, and just forgot it. Old people do,' he added gloomily.

'I shouldn't think Viola could have got up there,' said Greg. 'Anyway, I've never seen her smoke.'

'Well, your old girl, then,' said Warleigh. 'Or it was just the wiring. It often is in these old houses. And of course, being full of paper—dry old stuff, too, the worst thing there is—the whole thing must have caught in no time. Everything up there's a complete write-off, and most of the first floor's in pretty bad shape. I doubt the other old thing will be moving back there for many a long month.'

'Desmond,' said Margaret Seymour-Strachey, 'you've got to get her back into that house as soon as possible. She'll drive me mad if she's not out of here soon.'

They were in their living-room, furnished with superbly anonymous taste, and looking out on the double garage and the green lawn and the spring flowers, tastefully clustered. Her husband looked at her with annoyance in his cold blue eyes, his thin lips pursed in an expression she knew very well.

'That's nonsense, Margaret. She's only been here a day. You know what we agreed.'

'We agreed to keep an eye on her and stop Hilary jumping the gun on us. I certainly never agreed to be treated like an under-housemaid of the eighteen nineties.'

'But after all, she's naturally upset.'

'Perhaps she is, but she's trading on it. And if I know her she'll go on trading on it. Last time I went up she asked for a little bell, so she could ring for me. It's no joke, Des. And I don't like her being near the children.'

'You're talking of her as if she were an infectious disease.'

'I speak as I find. She's a bad influence. She sets them against us, and she puts strange ideas in their heads. Just the way she cuddles · them the whole time—it's disgusting.'

'You're upset, Margaret. Overwrought. Things will settle down after a while.'

'I wouldn't mind so much if they were girls . . .'

'You've got to remember there's money involved.'

Margaret Seymour-Strachey looked up into her husband's hungry, hawkish face, with its open calculation. Money, and a pleasure in using it ostentatiously, was one of the bonds that held the marriage together. Drab herself, Margaret loved having people in and letting them notice their new possessions. But there were limits.

'The downstairs was hardly damaged at all,' she said, obstinately. 'The house is insured with the Northern. What's the point of working for them if you haven't got the pull to get that done? I want work started on that house by the end of next week.'

Desmond was one of those dominant husbands who knew that on one or two issues he faced adamantine resistance, and understood when to give in. 'All right,' he said. 'I'll do my best. But it'll look very odd if we rush it too much.'

'Odd?'

'Suspicious. I mean, she'll think that—'

'Desmond!' His wife's voice, high and urgent, stopped him in mid-sentence. She was looking down to the garden gate, which at that moment Greg Hocking was closing carefully behind him.

'It's your mother's fancy man,' said Margaret Seymour-Strachey, in tones of intense revulsion.

'Yes?' said Margaret at the front door, with an attempt at a friendly smile, which somehow turned out cold, like an arctic summer.

'I'm sorry to bother you, Mrs Seymour-Strachey,' said Greg, in his best dealing-with-difficult-parents voice. 'I realize this is a pretty terrible time for you, and I don't want to butt in. I just wanted to ask after Mrs Machin.'

Margaret Seymour-Strachey thawed slightly. She had heard about Greg from her mother-in-law, and had conceived various lively suspicions. Disgusting, she had thought to herself. But still—one had to keep an open mind, didn't one? He looked a pleasant enough young man, and genuinely concerned. 'Ah, you must be—'

'Hocking,' said Greg, 'Greg Hocking.'

'That's right. I've heard so much about you, from Mother. And you were a very good friend to poor Hilda, too, weren't you? We're all *so* distressed about her. It seems impossible, doesn't it? She was so full of life. Just like Mother, really.'

'Is Mrs Machin recovered today? I wondered—'

'Yes, of course—you'd like to see her. I'm sure she'll love that. Won't you come in?'

Chatting brightly, Margaret led the way upstairs. While Greg waited on the landing she knocked on one of the bedroom doors. Without waiting for a reply, she put her head into the room and said in that all-things-bright-and-beautiful voice she reserved for her mother-in-law, which Greg found grating even on first acquaintance: 'I've got a lovely surprise for you, Mother dear. Just guess who's come to pay you a little visit!'

'I saw him come up the path,' said an angry voice. 'Have you asked him to take off his coat?'

'No—I didn't know how long you ought—'

'Then please take it down and hang in it the hall. Ah, Gregory—' She received him grandly, seated in an armchair specially moved into the bedroom. 'Bring us tea—a *pot* of tea, and was that a sponge I smelt cook-

ing earlier? That will do. And biscuits, but not those
packaged chocolate ones, please. The Dalton service.'
Greg, who had retreated to the window in embarrassment, heard her hiss in conclusion: 'And next time,
ask first before you bring anyone up.'

Viola Machin, clearly, had recovered from the
shocks of last night. Pimpernel, it was true, was looking less than his usual yappy self—a smoky smell hung
around him, and he lay gloomily on the bed, a chas-
tened dog. But Viola had reassumed all her wonted,
iron-clad voluptuousness, and only her reddened
eyes—had they, Greg wondered, been rubbed since she
saw him coming up the path?—suggested that she
might have gone through a frightening or saddening
time. Her mood as she made Greg at home veered between hostessy (and frankly womanly) pleasure at
seeing him, and a desire to convey a sense of fragility
and grief, which pretty clearly she did not feel.

'I know you didn't come to be thanked, Gregory,'
she said, motioning him into the other chair, 'but
thanked you must be. You were most kind, most helpful last night. Just when I needed it most, too.' She
leaned forward and put her hand on Greg's thigh.
'And I want to thank you on Hilda's behalf. I've
heard all about it. I know you did everything you
could. Poor, poor Hilda.'

It was the second time in their acquaintanceship
that she had put her hand on his thigh. It was becoming a habit, and might in time become a tradition. It
was not easy, either, to withdraw one's leg when sitting down. The hand had the warmth of personal
feeling, whereas the theatrical sigh with which she
said her last words was nothing but an actressy trick
from a bad radio play. Greg was panicked into opening too baldy the subject closest to his heart.

'I've been wondering about how she died,' he said.
'An accident. She fell and hit her head,' said Viola

abruptly, withdrawing her hand. Then, turning on the tap marked 'emotion', she went on: 'Such a terrible end, but quite sudden, I think. She must have panicked when she first smelt the fire. And I was *there* still—downstairs—asleep. I knew nothing about it. The thought will haunt me as long as I live.'

Irritated by Viola's habit of slipping into clichés from the West End plays of her youth every time feeling was called for, Greg said: 'You'd seen her earlier in the evening, hadn't you?'

There was a pause.

'Yes. Yes, I had,' said Viola. She now looked ahead with graceful pensiveness. 'I'll tell you something I've told no one else, Gregory. We had words.' She knows they must have been overheard, thought Greg. 'That's what makes my memory of last night so—so terribly hard to bear. It torments me. You know we *did*, now and then. Have words. It was natural, really, and it meant nothing—nothing at all. But that *that* should be my last memory of her! And who knows?—perhaps she was still upset when she smelt the fire. Perhaps that's why she panicked.'

This aspect was being over-insisted upon, Greg thought, and he said: 'I don't associate Hilda with panic.'

'Oh—we women,' said Viola vaguely. 'Ah, tea.'

She allowed Margaret Seymour-Strachey to bring in the tea things and set them out on the bedside table without speaking further. Her daughter-in-law was forced to chat on brightly to Greg about whether the sponge had turned out well, and whether Greg liked ginger nuts. She was, Greg thought, suppressing considerable irritation with difficulty. 'I'll leave you two alone to chat,' she said at the door.

Before she had time to close it, Viola said loudly: 'Much too strong. She knows that's not how I like it.'

She had not, in fact, begun to pour. Seeing Greg's

eyes on the untouched teapot, she said, almost roguishly: 'Ah, you've caught me out. What a detective you'd
make. And now you're saying to yourself: "What a
disagreeable woman." '

'Not at all,' murmured Greg, like a schoolboy de-
tected eating sweets under the desk. 'None of my
business.'

'But there are reasons, you see. I'm not doing it
just to be difficult. My daughter-in-law has never liked
me. She's so conventional, you know. Young people
often are these days, I find. She thinks I'm a wicked
woman. Really! She's such a *cold* person, and I'm so
warm. Those poor children. I have only to kiss them,
my own grandchildren, and she calls them away. My
heart bleeds for them, literally bleeds! They're
growing up emotionally deprived!'

In the pause she poured Greg's tea, which was not
at all strong, and handed it to him. Then she said:
'So you see, I'm making myself as unpleasant as I
can—and I assure you I can!—to make them want to
get rid of me as soon as possible.'

'What do you mean—get you into a home or—'

'A home! A *home*!' Viola nearly shrieked. 'Can you
imagine ME in a HOME?' Greg blenched before the
tempest had had stupidly unleashed, but Viola quiet-
ened down as he murmured apologies. 'Did *she* say
anything about a home on the way up?'

'No, no, really, it was my silly fault, I—'

'They'd better not try it! No, you see, my son Desmond is in insurance. The house was covered by his
firm. He can get things done, if he shifts his—shifts
himself. I want workmen into that house as soon as
possible, and I want to be back in it the moment it's
habitable. I refuse to sit on in this house and be
treated like Christopher Robin by *her*.'

In the pause that followed Viola said with decep-
tive sweetness: 'Do have a piece of that dreadful

sponge, Gregory. I shall take a bite and leave the rest on my plate.'

'May I ask you what you had words about?' said Greg, biting into the excellent sponge.

'Oh, you know—' said Viola, with her theatrical sigh. She clearly had hoped the subject had lapsed. 'The old things. Old battles, and old soldiers fighting them over again. She suggested in that shoddy little newspaper interview that I'd broken up her marriage. . . . but let's not talk of it, Gregory, please. I shall only speak ill of the dead, and regret it afterwards.'

Greg Hocking was tempted to say: At least she'll never get her side of the story across now. Instead, more tentatively, he said: 'I suppose Hilda had given anything she had of interest to Mr Kronweiser before she died.'

'No doubt,' said Viola sourly. 'She was going to him with letters right to the end.' She caught the drift of his thinking, switched on an open smile as if to compliment him on his loyalty, and said: 'I think you'll find Hilda's part in my husband's life put *perfectly* fairly when Mr Kronweiser's book comes out.'

'I'm sure, I'm sure,' said Greg hastily. Why did he always feel so intimidated by Viola Machin? She did something to a man: made him feel about six, and caught with a warm jam puff from the kitchen table. His eye, coasting with embarrassment round the room, fell on a letter from Jackson's, the publishers. Out of the blue he said: 'I only wish she could still be alive to enjoy it. The fuss, I mean, and the money. She would have enjoyed having a bit of extra money.'

'She would,' agreed Viola. 'And of course we had our little agreement about the second book. She looked after her interests, you know. There was no putting anything over our Hilda, oh no. Not of course that I'd want to.'

'That will go to—who, do you think?'

'That chit of a daughter, I imagine. A rather sharp creature I always thought, but there. Of course I shall honour our agreement to the letter. Not that the money will amount to much. You mustn't imagine anyone gets rich from books these days, Gregory. But if it lasts it will be a nice little bit of pocket-money for her.'

But *how* much? Greg Hocking wondered.

'I won't ask you to have another piece of sponge, Gregory,' said Viola. 'It would only encourage her.'

Taking this to be a form of dismissal, Greg stood up and prepared to take his leave.

'How considerate of you,' said Viola, clearly not loath to see him go. 'You understand I shouldn't be tired.' She struggled to her feet to see him to the door. As she did so, Greg's eye went back to the letter on the dressing-table. He caught the words 'American rights' and 'four thousand pounds'. Then he allowed Viola to show him out to the landing.

'I hope you'll be at the funeral,' said Viola in her grand way, as if it were her show and there'd be cocktails afterwards. 'I *hope* to be there myself. I *will* be if I have the strength. But I don't know what the doctor will say.'

Downstairs in the hall Greg took his coat, and was going to let himself out when he was forestalled by Viola's son, who came out from the sitting-room, his wife hanging back in the doorway.

'We haven't met,' he said, with a formal smile on his face, and holding out his hand. 'I'm Desmond Seymour-Strachey.' Greg was first impressed by the handsome face with its lean, almost sunken outlines. Then he saw the watchful, ruthless, dissatisfied eyes. The sort of man who takes an old woman for everything she has. Not that he'd have a chance with Viola.

'I'm glad your mother is feeling better,' he said. 'It

must have been a terrible experience, at her age. But she seems to have come through it very well.'

'We're deeply grateful to you for your interest,' said Desmond. 'Both of us, my wife and I. Yes, she does seem to have weathered things remarkably well. But we're worried a bit about her state of mind. She seems a little—well, odd. We feel it may have upset her mentally. Did she say anything—odd to you?'

'Nothing at all,' said Greg, letting himself out of the front door. 'She seemed to have things well under control.'

But *what*, he thought, as he closed the door behind him, did they think she might have been saying?

CHAPTER X

STRATEGIES

'You aren't happy, Greg, are you?' his girl-friend Helen asked him.

Since they were in bed the query was ambiguous, and might have had reference to what had gone before. Greg, however, understood her perfectly well.

'No, I'm not,' he said, gazing up to the ceiling, to which he was sending little puffs of cigarette smoke. 'It's this damned Machin business.'

'*Is* it a business?' asked Helen. 'Isn't it just a fire, with an old woman dying? After all, it happens all the time in these old houses.'

'Granted,' said Greg. He sat up in bed, stubbed his cigarette out, and put his arms around his knees in thought. 'Look,' he said: 'I'll tell you the sum total of why I'm uneasy about it—and I tell you I *realize* it sounds pretty feeble. That's what makes it so frustrating. First, most of the fires where old people die happen at night. It wasn't half past nine when this one started, and neither of the old women in the house was in bed. Second, on any other night Hilda might have dozed off in the chair, but not after she'd had a flaming row with Viola.'

'The other one did.'

'OK, Viola did, but she's different. A row was all in a day's work for her, and at the end she'd feel pleased with herself and at peace with the world. Hilda might

have enjoyed it while it lasted, but at the end she'd
have felt upset.'

'Yes, I'd agree with that, from what little I knew of
her,' said Helen. 'That is, if it was a row, not a spar-
ring match—that wouldn't have worried her at all.'

'It was a row. Then—what happened afterwards:
she panics, everyone says. I've never known anyone
less likely to panic than Hilda. And the fire was only
in its early stages by then, remember. She grabs her
handbag and rushes along the landing, and she
falls—so hard, they say, that she has a nasty long
wound on the back of her head. Can you imagine it—
a light little body like Hilda?'

Helen sat up in bed beside him and thought. 'Just
one thing you said, though, Greg: the fire was in its
early stages. OK, but if it was a lot of old papers and
stuff in the attic that was burning—old letters and
manuscripts and stuff—there might be a hell of a lot
of smoke, mightn't there? And *that* could easily have
panicked her.'

'Granted,' said Greg. 'But if that was the case I
don't see that she could have *rushed*. You couldn't,
through thick smoke, however much you wanted to.
And if she didn't rush, how come she fell so heavily
as to make that sort of wound? I know I sound like a
bloody know-all, but all I can say is, if that satisfies
the police doctor, it doesn't satisfy me.'

Helen put her arm round his waist, and for a moment they were silent and companionable.

'Anything else?' she asked.

'Oh—nothing tangible. The fact that it all seems to
come so pat: on top of the row with Viola, just after
the publication of the book, just when the second
book was going to bring her a lot of money. Old Warleigh would laugh his head off if I put reasons like
that to him. Perhaps he'd be right.'

'But say we accept what you're obviously driving at, who might have wanted her dead?'

'Viola, obviously. Her daughter Rose or her husband—for financial reasons. Either of the Machin boys—because it might be possible to cut Rose out of the agreement about book royalties. That Desmond, I'm pretty sure, has an eye for money.'

'But is the money enough? As a motive for murder?'

'It's enough if you want it enough.'

Greg got up, blundered round the tiny bedroom, and then went to the bathroom and showered noisily, as if he were trying to knock sense into his head. Later, as he was dressing and Helen was in the kitchen frying bacon, he shouted: 'You see, it adds up to nothing. I'm ashamed of myself.'

'But you're going to do something about it?' came back Helen's voice. He looked around the door into the kitchen. She was a small, tough girl—determined, opinionated, with light brown hair and quick, sharp eyes. She had thrown on an old dress and not much else, and she played with the frying-pan as if it were Pancake Day.

She looked adorable. Eatable.

'Oh yes,' he said. 'I'm going to do something about it.'

Greg Hocking was one of those rare people who drift into teaching and find themselves, to their own surprise, absolutely cut out for the job. At school he had been enthusiastic but undistinguished, and after it he had found himself in a polytechnic in the Midlands, in the state of paralysis of the imagination that tends to grip adolescents when the time for choosing a career looms. He had sampled English, which was taught by doctrinaire young men with fuzzy hair-dos and a weakness for the polysyllabic. He had decided

it was not a subject for honest men, and had gone on
to history, where he had developed a real interest in
local history and a talent for getting old working-class
men and women talking about the customs and social
conditions of their childhood. It was this talent which
had landed him the job with the Oswaldston College
of Further Education and he was already unearthing
long-forgotten aspects of Lancashire social history,
and writing about them in the local paper.

His girl-friend Helen was Lancashire born: she too
had drifted, but into secretarial school. She had
stayed there, always conscious that she was preparing
herself for an existence of unutterable boredom, and
was one of an enormous number of women who were
training themselves for an 'if I don't marry' life. She
had drilled herself to super-efficiency and had become
one of the very highly paid temps the advertisements
talk about, because there seemed little point in such
jobs unless they were extravagantly rewarded. After a
few months she had decided that anything would be
better than the ever-changing impersonality of that
sort of life. She had taken a job in Manchester which
bored her as much as she knew it would, but where
she could settle down and get to know the people she
was working with.

She had met Greg at a film-club meeting, where
they had laughed through a leaden documentary on
Cuba. They were similar types: happy, uncompli-
cated, but with an undercurrent of seriousness that
made them want to take different directions, see with
their own eyes, not other people's. They both hated
orthodoxies and band-wagons, catch-phrases and rally-
ing-cries. At the moment their relationship was a
weekend one, but both of them occasionally thought
that the idea of marriage still had something to be
said in its favour.

As they sat at breakfast, eating a meal hearty even

by North Country standards, both of them chewed
over more than their fried goodies. Finally Helen,
pushing back a plate that still had half a bready
sausage on it, said: 'So what we need now is a plan of
campaign then, isn't it?'

'Yes,' said Greg, 'of independent action.'

'Independent, of course,' said Helen. 'But your
being pals with the local superintendent isn't going to
do any harm.'

'On the contrary,' said Greg. 'As far as I could
judge, he thought me an incompetent idiot who
ought to be minding his own business. I don't suppose policemen like being taught their jobs any more
than the rest of us do. The most I can hope for is
that I might meet him over a pint and get him to be
indiscreet—tell me if there is any dirt on Desmond
Seymour-Strachey, for example.'

'Did you take against him? He seems to be your
prime candidate. I haven't met him. What's he like?'

'Voracious. Greedy for more. And not a scruple in
his head about how he gets it, I'd guess.'

'Then we put him and Viola at the top of the list,
do we? Who goes on it next?'

'Well, Rose the daughter, I suppose, and her husband. He's a deadly dull little man as far as I can see.
Wouldn't have the guts, you'd say. But then, you'd
have said the same about Crippen or Christie, wouldn't
you? Then Viola's other son: open, jolly chap, always
laughing. Again, not the type you'd think. But it's a
selfish family, I'd say. They take what they want. I'd
keep him well in the running. Then of course there's
Desmond's wife—I'd forgotten her. I didn't get much
of an impression of her. I'd like to look at her background. Then I suppose Kronweiser was always
around the house—but there's no motive there.'

'That little fat body we saw in the pub one night?

He looked a right pill. I saw him in Manchester the other day, all hot and greasy and suspicious.'

'What was he doing?'

'Coming out of the office place opposite where I work. He walks like a constipated duck. I'd know him anywhere.'

'Well, that's the cast-list, as far as I know it. Of course there could be plenty of others I know nothing about.'

'And then there's the question of motive and opportunity, I suppose, isn't there?'

'Exactly. The two obvious motives are either money, or just plain dislike and jealousy. If it's money that's at the root of it, it's going to be hellish difficult to get the details.'

'And if it's just personal feeling, it's difficult to see why it should happen *now*. You're thinking, after all, of Viola Machin, aren't you? But she and Hilda have been living together for years.'

'True. But you've got to remember that it's *now* that the whole question of Walter Machin has come up again—because of the new interest in him, and the republishing of the books and so on. So the pair of them have probably been mulling over all the old grievances—in their minds, if not openly.'

'The old grievances . . .' said Helen, thoughtfully. 'We know so little about them. What were they? The rivalry over Walter, and the fact that Viola took him from Hilda some time during the war or just after?'

'It must be that, mainly.'

'It's very slight, isn't it Greg? I mean, after so long a time. And of course it mainly works the other way, doesn't it—I mean Hilda hating Viola.'

'Viola says she got mad about that interview in the paper, about marriages being broken up.'

'But that's much too slight, surely, Greg?'

'Combined with the rest—'

'But the rest is Hilda's grievance, not Viola's. There just *must* be something more.'

'I think you're right,' said Greg thoughtfully. 'A whole lot more. The problem is that it probably all lies in the past—thirty, forty years back, if it's Walter Machin that's at the heart of it, as I begin to think it could be. It's going to be the very devil to disentangle at this late date.'

'There must be a lot of people around who still remember him well.'

'I see ahead of me,' said Greg melodramatically, waving a piece of toast and marmalade, 'hours and hours of interviewing old-age pensioners in pubs.'

'Well, that's in your line. That's exactly what you find interesting.'

'They *always* expect you to buy them drinks. Get the cheaper cuts of meat for the weekends from now on.'

'Isn't there anyone else you could ask—closer?'

'His daughter would hardly have known him—and anyway she's on my list. The Seymour-Strachey boys would remember him better—but so are they. Of course, there's their father.'

'Viola's first? What do you know about him?'

'Not much. I think they split up some time during the war. Wait a bit—Viola said he was a writer of some sort. I have the idea he was some kind of critic. The way Hilda talked gave me the idea they were all four fairly pally early on.'

'It might be worth talking to him, if he's still alive. Though he might have a grudge.'

'And he might have good cause to be grateful. Being married to Viola is not my idea of bliss unending.'

'Then there are the libraries and places like that.

Wouldn't you find out something about Walter Machin there?'

Greg's forehead creased in perplexity. 'Do you know, I just haven't a clue. I don't think he had much of a reputation: he was a nine days' wonder—if that—just before the war. I should think *that* wiped out any chance he had of people remembering him. I don't suppose I'd get anything from libraries that I don't know already from the Colour Supplement article, or the interviews. Still, I could go into Burnley and give it a try.'

'And there's his publishers.'

'That's right . . .' The shadow of a project flitted across the further reaches of Greg's mind. 'That's right. Both the old and the new ones. And the new ones, Jackson's, would know all about the money, wouldn't they?'

'They would,' said Helen sceptically. 'But whether they'd tell . . .'

'Anyway, so far it comes back to this: either it's a matter of money, or the whole thing revolves around the two women, and the character of Walter Machin.' Greg thought for a bit. 'Funny,' he said. 'I've been interested in Walter Machin right from the start.'

On Monday morning Greg had no classes before eleven, so he took the early bus to Burnley and went straight to the Public Library. The reference section he already knew from his work on local history—a long, narrow room, darker than the rest of the library by reason of the heaviness of the books and their respectable bindings. With a nervous swallow he bearded the formidable young lady at the desk at the head of the room: she had always struck him as the sort of librarian who would prefer to see all the desks in her domain empty and all the books permanently under lock and key.

'Contemporary writers,' she said, as if they bordered on the unmentionable. 'Was it biographical or critical material you wanted?'

'Well, biographical really I supp—'

'Biographical. Well, there are one or two things.' She led him down the side passage and pointed to a shelf. 'Is it anybody very well known?'

'Not terribly, really.'

'You could try *there*.' She stabbed a book with a dangerous index finger, and took herself back to her desk, to survey her class and see that no one had taken a whiff of pot while her attention had been distracted.

Greg took down *Twentieth Century Authors* and turned unhopefully to the M's. There he was! Machin, Walter [1910-1948]. But the entry was very brief—only four lines:

> North Country British novelist, author of *The Factory Whistle* [1939] and *Cotton Town* [1940], the latter a collection of short stories. Both deal with working-class life, and are in the Walter Greenwood tradition, though rather more ambitious in style and structure.

Not much of a haul, Greg thought. Nothing he didn't know already. On an impulse he turned to Seymour-Strachey. Nothing—nothing either under Se- or Str-. Clearly, as Viola had implied, not much of a writer. What other books might there be that could give him a bit of elementary information? He supposed he'd have to consult that formidable biddy at the desk.

As he made his way up, feeling like a schoolboy with skimped prep, his eye caught, with a start of surprise, the rotund shape of Mr Kronweiser, eyes darting suspiciously in all directions, working at a desk. Of course—his usual work-place had been burned

around his ears. He walked on up to the judgment
seat, and the librarian cast a disapproving pair of
spectacles in his direction.

'That was very helpful,' Greg stammered. 'But
there's another man—a writer too, but not very distin-
guished, I think. He may have gone into something
else later—' his mind ran rapidly over the likeli-
hoods—'publishing, a university—I just don't know.
But he's still alive, I think. Are there any specialist
reference books?'

The reference librarian looked somewhat contemptuous, as was indeed, Greg felt, her right.

'There are, of course,' she said severely, 'but if you
don't know he went into one or other, wouldn't it be
best to try something more general first?'

'*Who's Who* or something of that sort?'

'Precisely,' said the librarian, and marched down
the aisle with him once more. Greg noticed out of the
corner of his eye Mr Kronweiser waddling out
through the door, and thought he'd finished work
early for the day.

'It's out,' said the librarian, in elegiac tones, as if
he were a particularly prickly thorn in the path of
her life. She started walking magisterially among the
desks. 'Here,' she said at last, pointing to the desk
newly vacated by Dwight Kronweiser. Greg sank into
the leather warmed by his voluptuous posterior.

Who's Who had never been Greg's favourite reading but rather to his surprise, it came up trumps:

Seymour-Strachey, Gerald Harcourt; Professor of
English Literature, University of Grimsby, 1942-
74; b. 8th June 1904; s. of Stephen Seymour-
Strachey and Charlotte Butler; educ. Wellington
College, NZ and University of Melbourne. Publi-
cations: *Heterosexual Strain in Modern English
Literature*, *The Ern Malley Affair*, *Sins of My*

Old Age and Earlier. Recreations: walking, talking. Clubs; none, on principle.

That was all. Not much to go on. But at least, it seemed, he was alive, even if only just. That was something to be thankful for. Perhaps he should put him top of his visiting list: at his age, it might be urgent.

CHAPTER XI

GRAND OLD MAN

The switchboard operator at the University of Grimsby was firm but quite helpful. Professor Seymour-Strachey had been retired for some time now, and had left Grimsby. But, no—she had no objection to giving Greg his address and telephone number. He now lived, it seemed, in a small village on the Yorkshire/Lincolnshire border.

Greg thanked her and put the phone down. He decided to ring Seymour-Strachey later, about tea-time, when he might be presumed to be in. Since he had ten minutes of lunch-break left he strolled into the canteen and sat down with Hickson, one of his more elderly colleagues—an avuncular type, deep in local politics, and decidedly cynical about Greg's attempts to resuscitate an era of Oswaldston history long and thankfully closed. But Greg knew he would answer his questions about anyone local, for he knew everyone, and dearly loved to display his knowledge.

'Know anything about a chap called Desmond Seymour-Strachey?' he asked casually, after the usual preliminaries of cursing the weather, the students, and the teacher's lot.

'A bit,' said Hickson. 'Not my party, but he gets himself in with both lots. Why?'

'Chap I know,' lied Greg, 'had some dealings with him. Some insurance claim or other. Felt he got twisted somehow.'

'Wouldn't be surprised,' said Hickson. 'That's his reputation. Sails close to the wind. You've got to watch him, but I don't think he'd do anything obviously crooked. Much too smart for that. Keeps in with us too, does our Desmond.'

'Oh—how?'

'You know the ways—gets invited to council functions, writes letters of qualified support in the local paper, or just shows friendliness and interest. He's too smart to pretend to be Labour, but he makes sure we don't forget him. He'd send us all whisky at Christmas if it was worth his while, only these days it's hardly worth the risk.'

'You wouldn't think he was involved in any local corruption, or anything of that sort?'

'Local corruption? Come, come, lad—this isn't the North-East. We call it legitimate furthering of mutual interests here. I expect he knows all about it, that's for sure. His dad-in-law was a Markby—the big building contractors. They've had their share of what's going, and more. But as to being involved—he's never been part of the firm himself, so I doubt it.'

Greg pondered on this information during his teaching hours that occupied the remainder of the day. At about four he rang up the number given him for Gerald Seymour-Strachey, but he was answered by a not too refined woman's voice—a voice with a touch of the treacle tart in it, and a touch of the plain tart as well.

'Gerald? He's out, love, I'm sorry. Can I give him a message, or will you ring back?'

'Oh—well, he won't know me. My name is Hocking and I'm ringing from Oswaldston. I wondered if I could come over and see your h—see him some time?'

'Oh yes, that'll be all right, love. When will you come?'

'You're sure I'll be able to see him? It's a long trip, and I wouldn't want to do it for nothing.'

'Oh, he'll see you. He's lonely as hell, poor old bugger, and doesn't know what to do with his time. You know what it's like when they retire, don't you? He walks miles, just because he's no one to talk to and he's bored stiff. If I tell him when you're coming, he'll be here to meet you. I'd welcome it too—get him out of my hair for a bit.'

'Well, I have a half-day off Wednesday. I could be there by about four, Mrs—er—'

'Right-e-oh. He's not my husband, by the way. I know a better trick than that, any day of the week.'

For some reason she found what she had just said enormously funny, and exploded into the phone with a fruity laugh before putting down her receiver. She had rung off without asking Greg what his business was. On the whole, he thought to himself, perhaps it was just as well.

It was tea-time when Greg got to Borthwick, a tiny village with a pub, a shop, and the bare population to support them. He had borrowed a car from one of his colleagues, and he felt hot, sweaty and uncertain of himself, having had to spend more time mastering the crate's uncertain ways than in preparing himself for the meeting to come. The evening before he had procured from the local library a copy of Gerald Seymour-Strachey's essay in autobiography, but a quick flick through the index had assured him there was no mention of Walter Machin, and he hadn't had time to bone up on the details of the man himself's career. He was going into the interview blind.

In the garden of the cottage there was a woman weeding a rose-bed. She was buxom, and the rust-red pullover she wore was not designed to minimize the fact. She looked, in fact, blowzy but good-humoured,

and of an age which is usually politely said to be
around thirty-five. She smiled at him cheerily and
opened the gate as he got out of his car.

'Mr. Hocking?' she said. 'He's expecting you.
Pleased as Punch, like I thought. Excuse me not shak-
ing hands—' she looked down at her own hands, then
looked around the garden. 'I don't know why I
bother. It's not as though I'm stopping . . . Could
you find your way in, do you think? He's in the
study—straight through the hall, and then far door on
your right. Oh—and lad: pretend you're interested in
him—just for a bit, to start with. It'll make him
happy, and things will go easier if you do.'

Primed with the good advice, but uncertain how
far he could follow it, Greg went in through the hall
of the cottage, artificially created by modern alter-
ations, and knocked at the far door on the right.
Pleased as Punch at the thought of his visit Gerald
Seymour-Strachey might be, but the 'Come in' that
answered his knock was lordly. Greg pushed the door
and found himself in what must have been the largest
room in the cottage. Every inch of available wall
space was taken up with bookshelves, and every inch
of shelf-space was taken up with books—books, mostly,
with tattered jackets or sun-faded bindings and dating, Greg guessed, from the 'twenties, 'thirties and
'forties—presentation copies, review copies and re-
maindered copies among them. The room itself, however was perfectly neat, and provided an excellent
foil for Gerald Seymour-Strachey, who was no driv-
elling dotard, but a smart, upright, handsome old
man, his clothes admirably cut and suitable for the
occasion, his profile cunningly arranged to impress,
his mane of white hair, thick and shiny, suggesting in-
tellect and a sense of the aesthetically satisfying. He
was the Patriarch, the Fount of Wisdom, the man to
whom pilgrimages are made. Here I am, he seemed to

say, in the fullness of my years. Come sit at my feet and drink the wisdom learned of experience.

Only the desk, empty and sparsely furnished, suggested that he was a Patriarch with time on his hands, a Fount of Wisdom from whom too few cared to drink.

'Do sit down,' he said magisterially. 'Good of you to come. Mr—Hocking, was it?'

'That's right. Gregory Hocking,' said Greg, nervously sitting.

'A—a student, perhaps?' hazarded Gerald Seymour-Strachey, smiling benignly.

'I have been,' Greg allowed himself to say. 'English literature.'

'Ah yes,' said the Patriarch, opening out his hands in an expansive gesture. 'The teaching of English—it was a wonderful profession in my time. Of course, since—'

'It is since that I studied it,' said Greg.

'I saw it all happen,' said Seymour Strachey, leaning forward in a burst of confidentiality and exposing a set of amazingly white teeth. 'When I went to Grimsby, in the war, there was just me and a few students—invalided servicemen, some nice girlies just out of school—things were lovely. We tasted, we enjoyed, we discussed. Then the soldiers started coming back after the war, and we got new members of staff—earnest young men who got all intense about everything. Started chucking names around, made me feel I ought to read them. I read Leavis—it was like eating barbed wire. By the 'fifties we were taken over by Leavisites—ghastly neurotics shrieking about maturity. Then there were other names—Raymond Williams, someone with a name like a chamber pot, Fry—after a time I didn't even bother to learn the names.' He shook his head sadly. 'It's not a profession for a gentleman now. My God, I wonder what "Q" would say.'

Greg felt that it would be appropriate to leave a Remembrance Day silence in the room when he finished speaking.

'But I think of you as a *creative* writer,' he hazarded at last, amazed at his own effrontery.

'Nice of you,' said Gerald Seymour-Strachey, flashing at him those miraculously even teeth, and looking every inch the debonair squire of dames he must have been in his youth. 'Creative I wouldn't claim to be, but I've known them—lots of them.' His eyes dimmed. 'Upward, Douglas, Currey.' The dimness seemed appropriate. Greg had never heard of any of them.

'You knew Walter Machin too, didn't you?' he asked.

The eyes cleared, the relaxed body tightened, and Gerald Seymour-Strachey cast a glance at Greg almost quizzical. 'Ah yes—Walter. Everyone seems to be getting interested in him lately. I knew they would eventually. Yes, I knew him, and his wife too. See she died. Sad. Nice little woman.' He paused, seeming to survey the landscape of his relationship with the Machins. Then he said: 'Actually, as I suppose you know, I got rid of my first wife on to Walter.'

'Well—yes, I knew he married her after the war,' said Greg diplomatically.

'I tipped him the wink after I left her,' went on the Patriarch, with an expression of lubricious meditation. 'Told him there was Viola, waiting alone in London with no one to warm the bed up for her. And Bob's your uncle!'

'That was in—?'

'I left her in 'forty-three,' said Seymour-Strachey promptly. His face assumed an expression of sublime conceit, and once more he leaned forward with an air of confidentiality: 'I've married again since then, of course—married often.' He chuckled, in self-approbation: 'But it's always been *me* who left *them* . . .'

There seemed nothing to say to this. If Greg had understood the lady in the garden aright, Gerald Seymour-Strachey was in for a new experience. He was now, though, in a groove of reminiscence which seemed to please him mightily.

'We were alike in a lot of ways, Walter and I,' he said nodding happily. 'We both liked women. It marked us off, you might say—from the literary crowd, I mean. When Walter came up to London just before the war—those were times! Wot larks, as Joe Gargery says! And then during the war too, he had his fun. And I did too. I remember we met up in Grimsby, just after I got there—'forty-four it must have been. He insisted on calling me the Professor of French Letters—introduced me to everyone as that in the pubs. That was his sort of humour, you know. Tickled him no end when people took it seriously—I can hear his great golden laugh now.'

'So you remained friendly right through the war, did you?'

'Oh yes—right up to the end, you might say. I always intended to visit him after the war, but you know how it is: things were difficult, I was confoundedly busy at the University, I didn't particularly want to see Viola again—though you've got to swallow the pill with the jam, haven't you, and there was no particular reason why I *shouldn't* see her again. But then the next I heard he was dead. Life's like that, isn't it?'

'How did you meet up in the first place? Was it when his first book was published?'

'No, no—before.' Gerald Seymour-Strachey put himself in a self-conscious pose of memory, as if rehearsing for a television down-memory-lane programme. 'We met in a pub—back in, oh, 'thirty-seven, 'thirty-eight. Hilda and he were in London on a spree, Viola and

I had come out of the theatre for the interval—Noel Coward, Rattigan. I forget what. Anyway, we met up, and we never did get back for the last act. We clicked —all of us.'

'You mean Walter was—interested in your wife then?'

Gerald Seymour-Strachey looked at him with something close to outrage on his face: 'No, no—nothing of the kind. What minds you young people have. No—we just had a gay evening out. Later on we got talking, more seriously—about the North, the unemployment. And then Walter mentioned his book he'd written, or was writing, I forget which. He thought I might be useful, I suppose. I'd told him. I wrote the fiction criticism for *Time and Tide*.'

'Did you help him with it at all?'

'With the writing? Oh no. Walter didn't need that sort of help—wouldn't have welcomed it, either. But I told him the best publishers to try—the pink-ohs, you know. And when it came out I gave it a puff in my little rag, and made sure the others did the same. I had a bit of influence in those days.' The handsome old man chuckled in childish vanity.

'What was Walter Machin like, before the war?'

'The same as he always was—happy, open, full of jokes, lots of them terrible. Always ready for a game, particularly if there was a woman involved. He was so full of life, it was—well, you felt you could light your cigarette off him.'

'But he must have been very politically conscious as well—I mean *The Factory Whistle*—'

'Oh, he was, he was. Certainly. But he wasn't one of those bitter little bigots. He saw the humorous side—even of the slump. That's what marked Walter off. He enjoyed life, a hundred per cent, twenty-four hours a day. Lawrence kept saying he was living intensely with his whole body and all that, but Walter really did. And it gets into his writing. Read some of the short pieces—the one called "Lydia Horton and the Vile Seducers" for example. That's from life. That's the real Walter.'

'Why do you think his reputation didn't last?'

Gerald Seymour-Strachey leaned forward excitedly. 'Ah, but it did! In little pockets—that's nothing unusual, in the literary world. Why do you think these mentions of him kept cropping up over the years? People had been reading him, recommending the books to each other, lending them.'

'Yes, I see,' said Greg, feeling he was talking about a coterie that was way outside his usual sphere of research. 'But as far as the public at large was concerned, he was forgotten, wasn't he? For example, he was totally out of print.'

'I suppose so,' said Gerald Seymour Strachey, spreading his hands wide as if in despair at the fickleness of public taste. 'These things can't be explained. What do you think would happen if *Wuthering Heights* were published today? Three lines at the bottom of a column in the *TLS*. Even the feminist loonies wouldn't be interested in it. It would sink without trace. Well—something of the kind happened to Walter, after the initial interest.'

'I notice you didn't mention him in your autobiography . . .'

'*Sins of My Old Age and Earlier*? Good title, eh? Thought for a long time before I hit on that. Didn't sell as well as it ought to have, that book. What were you asking . . . ?'

'You didn't mention Walter Machin in—'

'Oh yes! No, well I didn't think anyone would be interested. Nobody was when I wrote it—four or five years ago—nobody *much* anyway. Now they've rediscovered him. He's the missing working-class novelist, the link between Lawrence and Sillitoe. If I were writing it now . . . I wonder if they'd be interested in putting out a revised edition?' He meditated, dubiously.

'But you do think Walter Machin was a major writer?'

'Eh? Oh yes, undoubtedly.'

'Why? What was it he—he *had?*'

Again Gerald Seymour-Strachey adopted a pose, this time pontifical. 'He never cut himself off from his class. He was one of the working-class, he stayed one of the working-class, and he drew his inspiration from the working-class.' He relaxed his pose and looked at Greg roguishly. 'That's the sort of thing one says at the end of lectures—especially now we have all those bed-sitter Marxists as students. Still, it's true enough. All the others left—went to Mexico, or Majorca, or Cambridge, or wherever, and wallowed in their guilt feelings. Walter stayed in the North, felt at home there, so his books are authentic—the real McCoy. That's why he'll live. Have a drink, m'boy?'

After a small glass of Cyprus sherry, Greg took his leave, amid pressing invitations to come back any time in the future when he felt like a chat. He would like to have gone more fully into the subject which was second in interest in his mind to Walter Machin—Viola Machin, and the way she had come by her second husband. But it looked like being a long, hot drive home, and he was teaching at nine on Thursday. At the door Gerald Seymour-Strachey said in his most patrician manner: 'I'd be glad if you'd let me know when Hilda Machin's funeral is. Like to send a wreath.'

'The inquest is tomorrow,' said Greg. 'I expect it will be soon after that.'

'Inquest? Oh yes, of course. Died in a fire, didn't

she? Have to in cases of that sort, I suppose. Terrible way to go, awful. But if you *could* let me know . . .'

'Of course,' said Greg. Turning back he said: 'What was she like when you knew her?'

'Hilda Machin? Bright little thing. Lively. Plenty of spunk. Gave him hell when he stepped out of line, I imagine. But made it up pretty quickly afterwards. Like they all do, eh, m'boy? Like all these women do.'

And laughing a laugh of benign condescension, Gerald Seymour-Strachey struck a pose of farewell against the doorway of his cottage. The final image he imprinted on Greg's mind was a handsome wreck, a St. Pancras Station of a man.

By the gate the Patriarch's buxom companion was still at work, weeding a not particularly fertile-looking patch of edging. She smiled and straightened as Greg approached and said: 'It looks as if you've cheered him up.'

'I hope so,' said Greg. 'He was very helpful.'

'He's got a fund of memories,' said the woman. 'Boring as hell, but still—if you're interested in that kind of thing it's all right I suppose.'

'He's remarkably spry,' said Greg, 'for a man of his age. Hasn't lost any of his faculties.'

'Not so you'd notice,' said the woman. 'I'm worried about what'll happen to him when I go.'

'Oh—you are going, then?'

'Too right I am. I'm not getting any younger. Can't throw my life away, can I? I need something with a bit more life.' It was not entirely clear whether she was complaining about her milieu or her companion. 'What I'd like would be for him to go back to that first wife of his.'

'Viola?'

'That's the one. I said the same to one of his boys when he was here.'

'It doesn't seem very likely. He doesn't talk of her with any affection.'

'Not to you, he wouldn't. That's his pride. If you'd heard him talk about her when he'd had a few you'd think different. You'd think the sun, moon and stars shone from her eyes.' She folded her arms over her ample bosom and completed her piece of Tin Pan Alley sentiment. 'If you ask me, she's the only woman in the world for him.'

CHAPTER XII

WALTER MACHIN'S DAUGHTER

The inquest was hardly more than a formality, the
verdict an inevitability. The coroner had not got
where he was by thinking, and he showed no inclina-
tion to start on this occasion. If the police said they
were satisfied that the death was accidental, that was
good enough for him, and should be good enough for
the jury. It was.

The due processes having been gone through, there
was nothing to prevent Hilda Machin being buried
according to the rites of the Christian church whose
doings she had cared remarkably little about during
her lifetime. Greg was extremely interested to see
whether Viola Machin would be represented in the
flesh or the flower at the interment, and he got permission from his Principal to take the morning off
and attend. 'You were good to the old thing during
her lifetime,' he said, 'so you may as well trot along.
It's all local history, isn't it? Oswaldston's going to be
living off Walter Machin for a few years.'

As it turned out, the Machins were there in force,
solemn in the church, gloomy by the graveside. It was
a chilly May day, with grey skies and a wind which
seemed thirsty for another death. Viola Machin, nevertheless, seemed impervious to it: she stood in
bosomy grief, in a becoming coat of umber shade,
dabbing her eyes at the pathetic bits of the service;
Desmond, in a heavy black coat, managed only an in-

surance agent's decorous grief; and Hilary looked as if cheerfulness might keep breaking through—which would probably, after all, be what Hilda would have liked most.

Rose seemed still to be genuinely upset. She had lost a good deal of her bloom and bounce, and looked as if the sentiments of the burial service kept stabbing her to the heart. Her husband, Bill Clough, seemed awkward and unsure of himself: his suit fitted badly, and he looked like a comic who has unwisely accepted a serious part in provincial rep. He continually looked around him, as if for advice, then dropped his eyes to his shoes. There was another relative from Hilda's side of the family with a feeble grasp on life and reality, who kept muttering remarks like 'To think she should be the first to go,' and 'Well, who would have thought it?' At the end of the ceremony she tottered off to the bus, looking as if she had every intention of popping in to the local when she got home and livening everyone up with a steady dropping of 'To think our 'Ilda should go before me' remarks.

When it was over Viola swept up to Rose, took her impulsively by the hand and murmured words of comfort. Rose showed signs of both anger and tears, and Viola swept on ahead towards the churchyard gate to avoid such an embarrassment. Desmond, after the briefest of mutters, hurried after her to tuck her into the car. Hilary lingered, and managed to seize on a moment when Bill Clough was talking to Greg to exchange his low words with Rose. It was odd, but Greg noticed Bill Clough's eyes following them sharply: he was saying nothing to the purpose so there was no reason why he shouldn't watch them, but Greg, following his lead, did wonder whether Hilary's mutterings were not of a rather different kind from

Desmond's. More—what? To the purpose? More *personal,* perhaps?

At the gate of the churchyard Rose turned to Greg.

'Would you like to come home for a drink? I didn't want to ask the others, because they were nothing to Mam. But she was fond of you—she'd like to think of us having a drink on her.'

'Thanks very much,' said Greg. 'I think I could manage a quick one.' Local history, he said to himself. Bill Clough bumbled around them, telling his wife she mustn't catch cold, and Greg had the notion that Rose's invitation had not been welcome. He stepped out of the short distance to the Clough home with added determination.

They were met at the front door by a delirious spaniel, who clearly had no idea of funeral decorum, and they proceeded into the front room, where Bill Clough switched on a bulging orangey imitation-coal electric fire, and then went to a horrible drinks cabinet—all plastic and flashing lights. The room seemed to speak nothing of Rose and everything of Bill—or was that, Greg wondered, just his own biased assumption? Rose went to fetch ice and tonic water from the kitchen.

'What'll you have, then?' asked Bill heartily, and then, with his odd alternations of mood on him: 'What'll it be?' quite mournfully, and looking bewildered at the array of bottles.

'A Scotch, please—plenty of soda,' said Greg, and settled down with it into the sofa.

'I must say I'd have been happier,' said Rose, when everyone was suited and they had all sunk into their chairs, 'if Viola had kept away. If I'd thought of it I'd have sent her a message: You won't be welcome.'

'Eh—that wouldn't have been on, Rose,' said her husband. 'You couldn't have done that.'

'I could have, and all,' said Rose. 'Or Hilary could

have kept her away.' Greg saw Bill Clough blink agitatedly and look sharply at his wife. She paid no attention to him. 'Everybody knows the two of them
had an almighty row that evening,' she went on. 'If
Mam was upset that night it was Viola's doing. She
should have had the decency to keep away. I nearly
choked when she came up afterwards.'

'What did she say?' asked Greg.

'"I miss her every moment of the day,"' quoted
Rose, imitating Viola's genteel contralto tones. '"I
know just how you must be feeling." Condescending
old bitch.'

'Of course, she probably does miss her,' said Greg,
to be fair. 'Old people miss their old opponents—
they've nothing to fight any longer.'

'If what I hear is true she's sharpening her claws
on her daughter-in-law these days,' said Rose.

Her husband, looking hard at his glass, said: 'You
ought to keep on the right side of her, any road.
There's the question of the money from the books.'

'Hmm,' said Rose doubtfully. 'Well, I have to admit that there she hasn't behaved too badly. We are
sharing the royalties—the same arrangement she and
Mam came to. That Desmond came round—she sent
him—and he discussed it with me. Right cheesed off
about it he seemed, too. That's probably why she sent
him—she knew it would cut him to the quick. That's
a nasty piece of goods.'

'You think he's out for what he can get?'

'I'm sure of it. Everyone knows that. He doesn't try
to hide it. That's why he's not doing so well at the
moment: people like you to put up *some* pretence
that you're interested in something other than money,
even if you are in the insurance business. It doesn't
occur to him to.'

''Appen he wants to get his hands on the money
from your dad's books,' said Bill Clough, looking

around him with eager interest, as if he had made a discovery.

'Of *course* he wants to get his hands on it,' sighed Rose, not bothering to look at him. 'But he won't as long as Viola is alive. And he hasn't the least idea of how much it will come to. I could tell that from the way he was fishing around—he got that panting, thirsty expression on his face. He does, you know, when money is in question.'

'Did you tell him anything?' asked Greg.

'Not on your life. I'm not fond of Viola, but I wouldn't want her murdered in her bed. He'd do it for ten quid, let alone for this little lot.'

'I didn't know you knew him so well,' said Bill Clough.

'I've heard all about him,' said Rose.

'Anyway, you don't know yourself what they'll bring in, do you, Rose, so you couldn't have told him anything?' said her husband after a pause, when his pathetic, bewildered-puppy air had intensified.

'Don't I ever,' said Rose, with her old energy. 'I talked to Mam before she died. They've sold American rights in both of the novels, film rights in *The Factory Whistle* and they're being translated into quite a few foreign languages. Viola and I will get several thousand each—and it'll go on."

'You never told me this,' said Bill plaintively.

'Didn't I?' said Rose, not as if *it* had slipped her mind, but as if *he* had. 'Still,' she went on, 'we shouldn't be talking about money.' She leaned over to Greg. 'I want to thank you for all you did for Mam. I never worried about her this last year, you know, because I knew you dropped in and kept an eye on her. It's meant a lot to me, and I know it did to her.'

Greg was once more conscious of Bill Clough's eye on him—watchful, anxious, distrustful. What's he afraid of, he wondered? What's he got against me? He said: 'I failed her, really, at the end. I was only down there at the Spinners', but I didn't get to her in time.'

'You couldn't have known. Nobody could,' said Rose. She sat hunched in thought.

'Ee, it's nobody's fault,' said Bill Clough, falsely cheerful. 'And she had a good life, when all's said.'

'She had a *hard* life,' said Rose sharply, not looking at him. 'It's no joke being left with a young child to bring up on your own. It wasn't *then,* specially.'

'How did it come about?' asked Greg, neatly insinuating his toe into the opening. 'Was it by mutual agreement? Had the marriage been breaking up before the war?'

'According to Mam, Viola went and grabbed him as soon as he was demobbed,' said Rose, smiling a little at the memory of Hilda's version. 'Manhandled him into her bed.'

'But there must have been something before that . . . ?'

'I suppose so. One thing Mam said suggested it had been going on for some time. . . . Years.'

'What was that?'

Rose continued looking down at her glass. 'I'd rather not say. . . . But, of course, Dad had had all sorts of minor affairs, and that hadn't broken up the marriage. Mam knew as well as anyone that he wasn't naturally monogamous.'

'I'll bet Viola made sure that he was,' said her husband, with feeling.

'Of course Mam said he never was the same after he married Viola. She would, naturally. He certainly never wrote anything more, so she was right to that extent. And there's stories around the town . . .'

'What sort of stories?' asked Greg.

'About her nagging, spying—you can guess. I'm not bothered about it myself. I hardly remember him, and I think what he did to our Mam was foul. Just when we were expecting him home—to phone and tell her like that. But I expect that was Viola's doing . . .'

'Some men are weak,' said Bill Clough sagely.

'I wonder how your mother could ever have come to live with Viola,' said Greg.

'Oh well—it was convenient, that was all. They met up because of the papers. Viola said she was going to sell the house, because it was too big for her (Hilary had just moved out), and she found the stairs difficult—so what was she to do with Walter's manuscripts and stuff, which were legally Mam's? Mam was just about to be rehoused by the council, and didn't fancy being so far out of town. So they moved in together. It was convenient, as I say. . . . Also, I think Mam kind of fancied the idea. . . . It was odd, sort of exciting.'

'Yes, that figures,' said Greg. 'That's what I thought must have made her do it.'

'You make your mam sound a right oddity,' protested Bill Clough. Rose ignored him.

'She'd been a bit bored,' she said. 'She'd had the odd little—well, not affair, exactly, but romance. But it wasn't anything much, because you had to be discreet in those days, specially if you had a child. It wasn't like now.' Her husband's gooseberry eyes shot in her direction, then looked at Greg, who lowered his noticing eyes to his knees and thus looked, if he could have seen himself, the picture of guilt. 'Then I'd moved out, when I had a job with a doctor in Blackburn, and she was very bored, I think. Moving in with Viola gave life a bit of spice, a bit of—danger. Well, not danger, of course, but you know what I mean.'

'Oh yes, I know,' said Greg.

'She'd have hated being in one of those old people's flats, and they're miles from the centre. She was a quarter of an hour away from us here, but still, from Viola's you can practically see this place. It made her feel more in touch.'

'Oh, can you see Meadowbanks from here?' asked Greg innocently. 'Did you see the fire? That must have been awful.'

'Oh no, I didn't see it. I didn't know anything till the police rang. You can't actually see the house quite. And I was in all the evening.'

'Not quite all evening,' said her husband. 'You took the dog out, remember. As usual.' The words seemed weighed carefully.

'Oh yes,' said Rose. 'I took Sally for a walk. But I didn't notice any smoke.'

But at the word 'walk' Sally had started putting up a tremendous performance, and the party broke up.

On the way back to the College Greg said to himself: That husband of hers is all het up about something. He's watching like a cat by a mousehole. He suspects something. And if those glances at me meant what they looked like, it could be plain old-fashioned sex. Or was there something else as well?

In the corridor of the College of Further Education Greg passed his Principal, who caught a whiff of his breath, and said: 'Funny thing: local history's the only subject I know that always seems to involve alcohol. Stick with it, Hocking my lad.'

CHAPTER XIII

WALTER MACHIN'S SON?

The Oswaldston Arts Club had an exhibition room, which they called the Lowry Gallery, in the upper storey of a disused warehouse not too far from the centre of town. The Arts Council sometimes sent round wispy collections of this and that, the Club had an exhibition of its own once a year, and now and then individual members had shows. The new renown of Walter Machin and the heady publicity which had resulted for the town in which he lived had suggested to the Arts Club committee (a mixture of the local genteel and the local far left) that a retrospective of the work of his stepson might neatly capitalize on the widespread interest.

Hilary Seymour-Strachey had readily agreed, for, though he had not his brother's absorbing and exclusive interest in money—still, he always had a use for it, and the thought was beginning to occur to him that he might soon have a woman and child to support, in addition to himself. He upped the price of all his unsold pictures by twenty-five per cent, borrowed a few old ones from their owners and painted some large, meretricious canvases to make a splash. The exhibition was ready.

Greg had seen the posters around for some days, and on the evening before opening day he made it his business to pass by the warehouse and go in, for he was a paid-up member of the club, and it seemed

easy enough to fake a mistake about the members'
viewing day. It was a hot May evening: the children
on the streets around the gallery were lightly clad
and quarrelsome, and the sunlight was streaming into
the upper room where the exhibition was displayed.
Greg went quietly up the stairs and saw Hilary Seymour-Strachey, in his shirt-sleeves, gazing, grunting,
altering positions, and generally acting like a first-
time mother.

It was, in fact, rather a delightful exhibition, and
Hilary was obviously rather delighted with it. Suddenly amid the grunts and petty adjustments there
would appear a great big smile on his face as he contemplated certain of the pictures. The ones that
pleased him most were in fact covert parodies of the
work of the committee members of the Oswaldston
Arts Club—the unconsciously phallic abstracts painted
by the vicar's wife (who would certainly stand in
front of Hilary's effort for some minutes and then
say: 'Now I find *this* one most *awfully* interesting'),
the screaming reds and oranges symbolizing revolutionary outrages of the local school-master, whose private life was as blameless as his politics were extreme.
Hilary's own pictures, the ones he took trouble over,
were all of Oswaldston, and took their colours from
its greys, dirty reds and beiges, their shapes from its
straight, monotonous streets and square houses. What
made them less than first-rate, yet also made them
popular locally, was the touch of theatricality and ex-
aggeration, the desire to impose, which was very foreign indeed to the character of Oswaldston as a town.

Greg stood in the doorway, and took in the man
and his work. Then, finding himself suddenly observed when Hilary swung round to compare one
canvas with another by the door, he coughed apolo-
getically and made a feint of backing out.

'I'm so sorry. I thought today was members' viewing day.'

'Tomorrow,' said Hilary abstractedly. 'Tomorrow the galahs descend, and squawk, and flutter their plumage.'

Then he went back to contemplation of one of his local scenes, his broad shoulders hunched in the vivid purple shirt, his head pressed forward. Greg thought he was going to fail in his object, and began to close the door, but suddenly, as if to prove the retentiveness of his painter's eye, Hilary turned round again to him, took a good look, and said: 'Weren't you the chap that was at the funeral? Hilda Machin's funeral?'

'That's right,' said Greg casually: 'I remember seeing you there.'

'Mother's mentioned you too. Didn't she get you to be go-between between her and Hilda?'

'Something of the sort,' admitted Greg.

'You carried some genteelly worded threat, I suppose? And some less genteel raspberry in reply, I imagine.'

'Actually, Hilda was quite co-operative,' said Greg. 'She wasn't any more anxious to spoil things than your mother.'

'What things? The great Machin revival? Well, naturally not. She got her packet out of it too. Not,' said Hilary, stroking his chin, with a quizzical, self-mocking smile on his face, 'that I can talk.' He gestured round the room expansively: 'I'm cashing in too, in my little way. The committee would never have given me this show if it wasn't for the Machin revival. Here—have a cup of tea?'

'Love one,' said Greg, and watched as Hilary went over to a little kettle on a hot-plate in the corner of the room and slopped boiling water over a tea-bag. On the way back with the dirty cup and the milkless liquid Hilary Seymour-Strachey once more looked around at his own exhibition with the expression of frank self-approval Greg had noticed before.

'Yes, as I say, the worthy burghers of Oswaldston would not have asked me to spread the artistic products of my maturity before their admiring gaze if it hadn't been for the Machin boom. They'd have registered the fact that I work for an advertising agency, and marked me accordingly: "I do think essentially he's a *popular* artist, don't you?" As it is, they'll go round with a wicked twinkle in their eyes, and say: "I *do* think he has some of the *verve*, some of the *sparkle* of Walter Machin, don't you, Alfred? Drag out the cheque book, darling." ' His imitations were good, but in the middle of the last one, something struck him, and he added afterwards: 'Almost as if he *was* my father.'

Greg was uncertain how to respond to this addendum, which did not seem to be addressed to him. Hilary, coming out of his reverie, noticed his discomfiture, and smiled as if it was something of not the slightest importance: 'The suggestion has been made,' he said.

'Really?' said Greg. 'Is it true?'

'Haven't the foggiest,' said Hilary cheerfully. 'I'd be the last person to know, wouldn't I? Actually, I wouldn't mind at all, because as far as I can make out Walter was an amiable scamp. And my real father—I mean my official, signed and sealed father—struck me the only time I met him as a grandiose old phoney. Still, it wouldn't do for me to go around claiming the authentic Machin genes. It might bring down on me the wrath of Motherdear.'

'They had known each other for some time before they married, though, hadn't they?' ventured Greg.

'Oh yes—years. They met some time in 'thirty-eight, I gather. Which rather rules out Walter as a father

for Desmond, since he was born in 'thirty-seven. Not
that anyone would ever think it, in any case: someone
like Horatio Bottomley would be far more likely. Or
was he earlier?'

'Do you remember much about Walter—I mean the
years when he was your step-father?'

'Not a great deal,' said Hilary. 'A bit of a card—
that's my impression of him now, as I say. But *then*—I
thought him marvellous as far as I can remember. I
was only five or six, and he was always playing, and
building things, and laughing. That's what I remember. But I also seem to remember rows, and Motherdear going on and on and on—she has that way, you
know: she just gets a subject, and worries it to death
and beyond, never giving up, like a dog with a dirty
old carcass. Anyway, then he got sick—and I don't
remember any more: he was upstairs, and we rarely
saw him. But I *do* remember that when we were
growing up, Mother never talked about him the way
she does now.'

'How do you mean?'

'Well, now it's all "Walter the great and good", like
Queen Victoria at Frogmore, or "Walter the great
writer, the neglected genius", like Mary Shelley.
Then it was "If I hadn't been *dragged* to this godfor-
saken town by that damned no-hoper that I married
. . ." and so on. The tone, you understand, has un-
dergone a subtle change.'

'So it seems,' said Greg. 'So you don't think the
marriage was a great success?'

'If you want my *opinion*,' said Hilary, 'and it's
nothing more, I'd say it was a multi-million-dollar fi-
asco. He never wrote anything after the war, you notice. I expect he found he'd sold his working-class
birthright for a mess of Bloomsbury pottage. He
probably found that Ma was good in bed, but hell as
soon as her feet touched the floor—and after all, even

Walter and Ma must have had to spend the larger part of the day vertical, I bet he ached to crawl back to Hilda, but Ma had him neatly encircled. Poor old bugger—he was probably glad when he got sick.'

'You don't like your mother, then?' asked Greg. Hilary threw back his head and laughed his great, frank, hearty laugh.

'Ma? We get on like a house on fire—now we no longer live together. We understand each other. I suppose your loyalties were to Hilda, weren't they? I wouldn't blame you. On the human level she was much the nicer of the two. But Ma is an original too. She's a cunning old thing, crafty as a rattlesnake—but she knows how to enjoy life too. That's why we understand each other.'

'She certainly seems to be enjoying life now,' said Greg—and then, realizing this was open to misunderstanding, he added: 'I don't mean now that Hilda is dead, of course—I just mean she's revelling in this revival of interest in Walter Machin.'

'She's lapping it up. She's got that unappetizing little Yank in tow, and she's feeding him the Authorized Version. That'll be even easier now Hilda's gone—no fear of the Devil writing a footnote or two. Then as the boom goes on she'll become the Professional Interviewee, the great literary relict. I've already heard her mention Woman's Hour, and wonder how to make contact. She'll probably write her memoirs: she always had a yen to be a writer, though her pen dribbles clichés. I can't imagine her letting the Kronweiser book be the last word.'

'He was an odd choice to write the book, wasn't he?'

'He was the first that came along. I expect she kicks herself for giving him those special facilities now, because it's sure to be one of those jaw-breaking pieces of unreadability Americans produce. What a jerk! Christ!'

'Agreed,' said Greg. 'He seems able to turn a pleasant pub into a speakeasy waiting for a raid. Not your mother's type at all, I'm afraid. Have you had much contact with him?'

'He was round to me at the office the other day, wondering if I had any letters. Why he imagined Walter would have written to me I can't think. Perhaps he'd heard the rumours. Anyway, of course I hadn't any. He went to Rose too, but her mother had given him any there were. Hey—give me that rag there.'

Hilary Seymour-Strachey grabbed the rag, and went over to a picture. He did something technical on it, and suddenly his attention seemed to revert entirely to his exhibition. Greg, after a perfunctory tour round the makeshift gallery decided he'd better slip off. He stood at the top of the stairs, looking back at Hilary chunky, lively, absorbed—and at his paintings.

What had he got from the talk? A view—conjectural but convincing—of the second Machin marriage. The suggestion (impossible to prove) that Hilary was not Gerald's son but Walter's. And then, looking back at the pictures—sharp, full of insight, yet somehow slightly flashy—he wondered whether, indirectly, they didn't give him the best notion he yet had got of Walter Machin himself.

Mr Kronweiser sat on his bed in the little working-class backstreet in Oswaldston where he rented a room, hunched forward and staring ahead. His paunch flapped up and down like jelly in a windy picnic, and his Adam's apple did a jig in sympathy. Kronweiser was thinking.

Dwight Kronweiser had been born in nineteen
forty-five, and had been named after the victorious
Allied Commander in Europe, whom his parents,
even then, foresaw as a future President of the
United States, a new Ulysses S. Grant. In point of fact
little Dwight (a chubby child, the offspring of
shopkeepers, who bribed him with trash food every
time he seemed to want to divert their attention from
the business of making money) turned out to be one
of Kennedy's children—for even in his teens he knew
a rising star when he saw one. When that particular
shooting star was shot he became an anti-Vietnam war
protester, a Chicago convention activist, one of the
young people who campaigned vociferously for
George McGovern (though, like everyone else, he actually voted for Nixon). He was a hippie when hip-
piedom was in fashion: he grew his hair long and
then (when people began to give up their seats to
him on buses, under the impression that he was a
pregnant girl) he grew a straggly beard as a decla-
ration of sex. He had experimented with drugs, but
in the privacy of his own home, so as to be able to say
that he had: after all, you never knew what you
might say and do under the influence of drugs.

He knew, in short, precisely when to take two steps
to the right, or one to the left. In academic terms he
sensed the changes in the wind so well that he knew
exactly when to stop dropping the name Marcuse and
start dropping the name Goldmann, when to switch
from expressing genuine enthusiasm for Black Studies
to expressing genuine enthusiasm for women's literature. He was a highly sensitized instrument, a finely
tuned social and academic barometer. His colleagues
and aspiring rivals watched him closely, measuring
themselves by him and running breathlessly after in
the directions he took.

Mr Kronweiser had just had a letter from his departmental head, a man whose word made or marred men's careers, a man almost as sensitive to fashionable currents as roly-poly Dwight himself. His letter was hearty, breezy, man-to-man: let it never be thought, it seemed to say, that I am the man who can put your academic career on the chopping block by a couple of words in the right places—BUT DON'T YOU FORGET IT! It was a letter that was meant to be scrutinized carefully for whispers of concealed meanings.

You sure seem to be on to a good thing with this Walter Machin [the letter said]. Trust you, Dwight, to pick a winner, and pick him before the rest of us have heard of him! I see Scribners is bringing out both the novels, and has a sizeable publicity campaign on the stocks. And I hear on the grapevine Trumphauser at Cornell is giving him a chapter to himself in his book on British working-class literature. If you can get your book out in reasonable time I can see it being a real winner, and position-wise it won't do you any harm, that's for sure. I know the Faculty as a whole appreciates your stature as pioneer in this particular area of the field, Dwight, and if you can consolidate your position as *the* Machin man, you should be a cinch for tenure. Best you be around, though, just to make sure people register you, because things sure are tight these days as you know, and new people spring up all the time like goddam mushrooms.

In a PS the man wrote: 'Too bad about the fire. I was going to suggest the library might make a bid for the MSS. Still, it was great that you had the transcripts done.'

Dwight Kronweiser too shook his head at the thought: if only there *could* have been a Machin Archive at the University of East Louisiana. But that was impossible. The important thing now was to decide what to do. The writing of the book was hardly more than half-way done, but did it *need* to be done here, ferchrissake? He'd soaked up atmosphere. as he had intended—my God he had. He'd soaked up all the motherfucking atmosphere he wanted, thank you very much. He'd tried all the local beers, piss-poor imitations in his opinion; he'd eaten tripe, and faggots, and dry pork pies in pubs. He'd walked up and down those shitawful streets, absorbing the sights and sounds and smells of the real Machinian Oswaldston, and he had tentatively rendered them in his mind in Brobdingnagian words. Wasn't that enough? The works were transcribed, the Walter Machin canon was established, the publicity machine was in motion, and would roll without him.

At home were hamburgers, and popcorn, Colonel Sanders's Kentucky chicken, Arby's roast-beef sandwiches, drive-in movies, seventeen television channels, all-night TV movies, and (last and least) his wife Jean. There was every reason to take off for home, and nothing he could see to stop him. And there was that last phrase in the letter—that one about new people popping up: he grabbed the letter and re-read that sentence, his eyes bulging with suspicion and fear.

It made up his mind for him. There was nothing to keep him here that could outweigh the thought of the possible conspiracies going on behind his back back home. No sir—the road led South, to Skytrain. He would settle accounts with his landlady, who hated his guts as much as he hated hers, then he would pack, then he would go home. He would leave this lousy dump. He was (if none of the mushroom men got in ahead of him) a man with a future in the University of East Louisiana. Nay—he was a man with a future in the U.S. academic world. He was the acknowledged High Priest of the Walter Machin cult.

CHAPTER XIV

THE WALTER MACHIN ARCHIVE

Greg Hocking had not been looking forward to ringing Jackson's the publishers about the Walter Machin papers. It wasn't his line of country at all. He had concocted all sorts of elaborate stories about why he wanted access, but things proved rather easier than he had expected. The telephonist at the other end was cheery and casual, and he was put through in no time to someone called Cyril Causeley, who, the girl said, was editor for the Walter Machin books.

'Oh, you're speaking from Oswaldston, eh?' said the very Southern, minor public-school voice. 'Fascinating! I keep telling myself I ought to go—with all this publicity that's blown up, and all that. But when it comes down to it, Oswaldston isn't the sort of place one visits, is it? what?'

Suppressing the divine ire of the Northerner at Southern superciliousness, which would hardly serve his turn at this juncture, Greg said: 'The point is, I've been commissioned by the local rag to write a pamphlet on Walter Machin and his World—'

'Oh, jolly good show,' burbled Mr Causeley.

'Of course I realize the papers are confidential—'

'Well, of course the new books are. We couldn't let you see them—'

'But I gather you have some of the correspondence—'

'That's right, and that's not really any of our

business. They're just duplicates deposited with us by this American chappie—'

'Kronweiser.'

'Something like that. I gather Mrs Viola Machin suggested they be left with us for safety, and for completeness' sake. I don't see why you shouldn't have access to those.'

'I'd be most grateful—'

'Of course the transcriber—this Yank—wanted it to be all very hush-hush and MI5, but I rang Mrs Machin myself, and checked up, and she said with all this new interest she thought the material ought to be available to any scholar who wanted to look at it. I think she'd rather gone off this Yank.'

'One would.'

Anyway, I take it you come under the heading of scholar, eh? what? So if you want to have a look, just pop along. Ask for me, will you? Nice to see a real Oswaldstonian—is that what you call yourselves? eh?'

Greg did not enlighten him about his real origins. If he was writing a bogus pamphlet, he might as well be a bogus native of Oswaldston to boot.

Two days later Greg was forced to attend the funeral of a dear aunt. His Principal looked at him suspiciously when he asked for the day off, and he stuttered, 'She brought me up, you know.' Consent was given in measured tones redolent of suspicion. I'm going to have to get better at lying, thought Greg.

He took the early train up to London. He was fortunate enough to have secured the nineteen forty volume of short stories from his local library. *The Factory Whistle* he had already read, in the handsome new edition personally inscribed to him by Viola Machin ('To Gregory Hocking—a very good friend to *both* Walter's widows—from Viola Machin'). The novel had interested him, but left him unsatisfied. There was grimness—dirt, undernourishment, deprivation—but no humour. Some of the descriptions of working-class life had been so strange, so remote from the Oswaldston that Greg had come to know, as to seem to belong to a foreign land, in a remote period of history. The fact was, he had not felt in the book the impress of Walter Machin's personality, as he had come to know it—or to think that he knew it.

He cast his eye down the contents page of *Cotton Town* and turned to the story that Gerald Seymour-Strachey had recommended; there it was, in the centre of the collection: 'Lydia Horton and the Vile Seducers'. The opening of the story leapt off the page with a vividness very different from that of *The Factory Whistle*.

> 'Pregnant!' said Lydia Horton, her face as horror-struck as if she were watching a Boris Karloff film. 'Ee, Doctor, I can't be.'
>
> 'Nevertheless,' said the doctor, 'that's what you are.'
>
> 'But I can't be. It's only happened once. Well, twice.'
>
> 'Well, I'm afraid the result is, you're pregnant.'
>
> 'But it's not *right*,' said Lydia Horton, looking around the dreary little back-street surgery in the least attractive part of Oswaldston as if it were part of her grievance. 'There's married people, they go for *months* and *months* without getting pregnant.'
>
> 'Well, you seem to have managed it in one. Or two,' said the doctor.

The piece went on to tell how Lydia, a sharp little eighteen-year-old mill-worker, who had fallen only twice, but unfortunately with two different blokes, finally got her man to the altar. Initially they both showed signs of running a mile and denying all knowledge, but by cunningly playing on their male pride, their desire to believe they were 'a better man' than their rival, she made each one mad with jealousy of the other, and finally had her pick of which she preferred, leading him up the aisle of the Methodist Chapel well before the bulge began to show.

It was a lively, salty story, vigorously told—a tap-room narrative, but with a tang of the real Oswaldston. Greg flicked back to the contents list. All the stories in the book were centered on people: 'Mrs Nussey and the Pawnbroker'; 'Jem Larkin and the Pools Win'; 'Peter Fairclough at Closing-Time'. It promised to be a microcosm of Lancashire life in the depressed 'thirties. He closed the book to look at the scenery of his native Cheshire hurtling by, but there was an expression of pleasurable anticipation on his face.

'It's nice to see a new generation reading Walter Machin,' said a voice from the opposite seat. Greg looked up to see an elderly man, with rimless glasses, droopy moustaches and a slight air of remoteness and authority.

'They're very good,' said Greg appreciatively. 'Very lively. I wonder they were ever forgotten.'

'They never were. Not by me, at any rate. I remember reading *The Factory Whistle* when it first came out. I'd been teaching in Preston it must have been three years then, and when I read that book I suddenly realized I knew nothing about Lancashire at all—not the real Lancashire. It told me things about life in the mills and factories I'd never have found out for myself in a thousand years. That one you've got there—*Cotton Town*—that came out just before I got called up. I kept it with me all through the war— Crete, North Africa. I read it every time I wanted to think of home—the tears used to come to my eyes.'

'It seems a very different world to me.'

'Oh, it would. It's a lost world now—lost as Conan Doyle's! When I got back from the war it was all gone—destroyed by full employment—not that I'm regretting *that,* you understand. But something went with it, too!'

'What was it he had that made him mean so much to you in the war?' asked Greg.

'Ee—he was a born story-teller. Just like a lot of these chaps in pubs. I'll tell you this, my lad: he made a Lancashire man out of me!'

At the next station he got out, and Greg settled down to read more of the stories.

Cyril Causeley, Walter Machin's editor at Jackson's, was hospitality itself. He was in his forties, wore a decrepit old blazer and flannels, and had rabbity teeth and a foolish expression. Only a sharp expression in the eyes suggested how he had made his way in the do-or-die world of modern publishing, where niceness gets you nowhere.

'Oh I say, wonderful to see you!' he said, bumbling forward and pointing his teeth in Greg's direction. 'Walter Machin's townsman, eh? Genuine article, what? Well, I found a little room for you—attic, I'm afraid, hope you don't mind—and I've put everything up there. Like to come along, eh? I'll show you the way—watch your step, it's a bit of a difficult climb.'

As they made their way up precipitous staircases and winding corridors, Mr Causeley went on talking: 'Remarkable this new interest in Machin. Not entirely unexpected, but still remarkable. Marvellous reviews for the reissue of his first book—expect you saw them. We've had tons of letters—you know the sort of thing: people who say they knew the originals of the characters in *Cotton Town,* people who say he said "bobbin-waggler" when he should have said "throcket shuttle". It all keeps the interest up! It's been quite fantastic. We're reprinting already.'

'How did you get on to him?' asked Greg, threading his bulky self through the labyrinth of curving stairs and looking towards his guide apprehensively. 'I mean, what was it made you decide to bring the books out again?'

A glint of bright intelligence appeared in Cyril Causeley's eyes as he stopped for a moment in his upward progress, and looked down at Greg: 'Ah, well— in this business you have to see the way the wind is blowing. What's in, what's out. Not just with the new things, but with the old as well. The student market— that's the one to get into. Not many people buy books nowadays, but students have to. So even if they haven't much money, they've no choice but to buy. What they want nowadays is stuff about the working-class—sociological stuff, of course, but also novels and plays. "The Working-Class in Literature"—that's the sort of course they want to take. Well, of course, you're in the racket, aren't you? You'd know all about that. Anyway, that's the sort of market we're aiming at. I say, here we are at last.'

He pulled open the door, and they came into a tiny attic, with several large piles of typescript, and several files, neatly set out on the table.

'This looks marvellous,' said Greg. 'You've really been very kind.' Then, unwilling to let the subject of the rediscovery of Walter Machin drop, he said: 'You were saying—about how you got on to him.'

'Ah yes, well, there's this market, you see, waiting to be supplied. And not just in Britain. Socially aware Scandinavians, earnest Germans, dotty revolutionary Italians—all wanting stuff on the working classes. *Especially* if it's written by one of them. Because if it's written by the bourgeoisie, it hasn't got the authentic whiff—what? So we were looking

around for interesting stuff to push—sounds like
drugs, eh?—he-he-he!—and someone mentions Walter
Machin. Genuinely working-class, writing in the 'thirties, when there's not as much interesting stuff as you
might think. Plugs a gap, you see? So we contact the
widow, take over the rights from the original publishers, and bingo! Then we find there's masses of stuff
still unpublished. Rapture redoubled! We start a big
publicity campaign (we're good at that), and now
we're raking it in!' He concluded his little lecture
with jovial self-approval, and then, standing by the
open door, he paused for a second and said: 'Sounds
cynical, all that, I suppose. Idealistic young chap like
you. And of course we're pleased as Punch to put him
in print again. We believe in him as much as anybody. Still, when all's said—we *are* in this to make
money! Cheery-pip!'

Left alone at the table, with the faint shadow of
daylight peering through the filthy window in the
sloping roof, and with a bare bulb in the wall behind
him, Greg looked at the piles of material before him,
and his heart sank. Oh, the exhaustive beavering of
Mr Kronweiser! Once settled into the unaccustomed
work, Greg found that things began to come more
into perspective. The greatest masses of material were
in fact the published fictional works of Walter
Machin: the yellowing typescripts of *The Factory
Whistle* and *Cotton Town*, retrieved from their original publishers, and a collection of miscellaneous stories and articles from newspapers which eventually
would be published in book form.

Most of this Greg felt he could ignore: either he
had read it, or could read it in more convenient cir-
cumstances. However, he tried some of the journalis-
tic pieces in what was to be the second posthumous
volume. They were all written in nineteen thirty-nine

or nineteen forty, and though they all concerned Walter Machin and his writing, or the industrial environment in which he lived and had grown up, they nevertheless contrived to be oddly impersonal and unrevealing. There was one piece of a mildly political nature: it had been contributed to the *Daily Herald* in October nineteen thirty-nine, and was called 'The Workers and the War'. The arguments had not stood the test of time too well, but it ended pithily enough: 'What the working man wants from the war is work.'

Putting this mass of stuff aside, Greg was left with two very manageable files filled with photocopies and carbon copies. One contained business matters of the sort that households—even households in the depression years—tend to accumulate over the years. There were gas and electricity bills, primitive hire-purchase agreements, insurance policies and such-like, all religiously photocopied by Mr Kronweiser. He had also managed to get hold of, and copy, all Machin's correspondence with Mattlock's, his original publishers. This started with a short note, dated October nineteen thirty-eight, agreeing to their terms for *The Factory Whistle*. For a time the correspondence was brief and businesslike, but it became more expansive after the book had received good reviews: there were thanks for entertainment, and enquiries about reprinting dates. The expansiveness came to an end in the middle of 1940, when he demanded better terms for *Cotton Town* than had been offered: 'The first book did well for you (for me too, I readily admit), and since I may soon be called up, and have a wife and child to support, I should like to leave them as well provided for as possible.' This request was refused, and the correspondence thereafter was perfunctory. Mattlock's business judgement was vindicated by *Cotton Town*'s sales: it only went into one printing. By the end of that same year Walter Machin was in

uniform. Thereafter there was no correspondence,
only a dribble of royalties statements, which ceased
entirely in '42.

The other file was of personal correspondence and
papers. Of this, comparatively little was from Walter
Machin himself, and some of these Greg had already
seen in the Sunday paper articles. There was a fairly
large number of letters about him, sent in the last few
months both to Jackson's and to Viola Machin by
people who had known him at one time or another.
There were schoolfriends, work-mates and (reading
between the lines) girls whom he had made love to
(who had, for the most part, sent their reminiscences
to Jackson's rather than to Viola). All these reminiscences told the same story: a big, healthy, gregari-
ous man, full of fun and sport, always living life to
the full and extracting from it all the juice it contained, and more. 'He could always make you tingle,
just being near him,' wrote one old woman who had
worked with him in Bury as a girl in 1929. 'Just a few
minutes alone with him was like a tonic. I only wish
there had been more like him in my life.'

Then there were letters to Walter, particularly
from his two wives. The first of those from Viola was
addressed in fact to 'Dear Walter and Hilda', but it
was not difficult to guess that it was intended primar-
ily for Walter's eyes. It was dated early in 1940:

> How is the war affecting you up there? Is is true
> there is more work to be had? If so, it's the only
> blessing I can discern in it. I am *convinced* it
> will be over in a matter of *months*. But if the
> worst comes to the worst and you are called up,
> Walter, remember there is always a spare bed-
> room here. Gerald seconds this warmly. He will
> not be called up, owing to his dicky heart (which
> I have never truly believed in until now, but

which turns out to be *genuine*). However, he has joined the fire service, and is called out most nights, so he too must be said to be doing his bit.

The other, even more revealing letter, was written early in 1945, after Walter had spent part of a long leave with Viola and the children (now alone, with divorce a matter of months away) in their London flat. The letter had not been shown to the newspaper men. Part of it read:

> The children talk about you all the time: when we are down in the shelter, which we still are, often, they keep saying they wish Uncle Walter was here, to make it entertaining. They miss you, Walter. You've become part of their lives. As you have of mine, darling. Sometimes I wake up at night, crying for loneliness. If I could only *know*—for certain—that you would be coming back to me as soon as this is over, I could bear it. Couldn't you *phone* me? I wouldn't press you for a decision, I promise you. I am not a nagging type, or possessive—even Gerald would admit that, I think. Above all I don't want to worry you: I'd feel like hell on earth if you crashed on a mission and I thought it might be my fault, even to the tiniest degree. But just to hear your voice, my darling—as the next best thing to having you here in bed beside me. Such a small thing for you, such a big one for me. *Try*, Walter, *please*.

This was the latest in date from Viola to Walter. If there were any subsequent ones, she had clearly felt them to be too revealing, too pathetic, or conceivably too shrill in tone to be shared even with Mr Kronweiser.

Hilda Machin's letters to her husband were unremarkable. Clearly they were not the sort of married couple that was used to communicating by letter, and when they did it was only rarely that anything illuminating was said. They were written either while he was on solo trips to London or elsewhere, or in the early days of the war when he was in the RAF. They contained news of Rose, details of life in wartime Oswaldston, stories from her daily work in teaching, which she had gone back to. They were, in fact, nothing but trivialities. Nor were the comparatively few letters of Walter Machin himself much more revealing. There were some letters to his mother, widowed and living in Bury—some phrases from which had been plundered for the article in the *Sunday Chronicle*. For the most part the letters were dutiful, full of domestic detail, and perfunctory. There were some brief notes to Rose—from Sheffield, Newcastle and other Northern towns. Only one of the letters was of any length: like the others it was typewritten, and was labelled by Mr Kronweiser: 'Given me by Mrs Hilda Machin, 21 April 1978.' It read:

> Mornington Hotel,
> Stephenson St., W.C. 1
> 2 June 1939

Dear Hilda,

Well, I got here all right! I'm at the same hotel as we stayed at last time—but it's not the same without you and Rosie. How's my girls? As you can imagine, I've been along to Mattlock's. They're twice as polite now—since that review in the *Observer*. They ask about the short stories as if they really *want* them—none of that toffee-nosed 'we might conceivably' stuff we had last time. They took me out to dinner too—lunch they called it. All sorts of things I didn't know how to eat. I thought: 'Well, you wanted a working-class original, and that's what you've got,' and I ate it all the best way I could—fingers and all. You should have seen their faces! Had a good pub-crawl last night. Everyone talking about war—jolly topic for a night out. 'Look on the bright side,' I kept saying: 'They'll need munitions.' Will go to Viola and Gerald tonight and hope they talk of something else. Have been walking around London all day. Was going through Admiralty Arch to the park when the King and Queen drove by! What guys! I had intended to go to Downing Street, but then I thought I couldn't bear it if old Chamberlain came out waving a bit of paper and smiling his death's head smile, so I just lay down in the park instead. I'll be with you on Sunday night, love. Love and kisses for Rosie, and tell her I'll bring her something good. What the hell *does* one buy for a two year old?

Love,
Walter.

It was the nearest Greg had come, he felt, to the real Walter Machin. The war letters, in comparison, were far less real and warm. As he closed the file, he was struck by an oddity of the collection: there were no love-letters from Walter to Viola. No letters at all. Had she never had any? Had she destroyed them in the period of bitterness towards Walter after his death? If so, she must be kicking herself now!

On the way out, Greg popped his head round the door of Cyril Causeley's office, to thank him.

'Oh I say, nothing at all. Really. You're welcome any time. Just wait till you read the second novel.

We're going to do marvellously with it. It's the real thing! Authentic!'

Greg forbore to ask how someone with an accent like that would know, and said instead: 'It'll bring in a tidy sum if it's a best-seller, I suppose.'

'An absolutely cracking sum! Marvellous thing for the two old ladies!'

'One,' said Greg.

'Oh, that's right. One died, didn't she? Well, that's the way the world goes, isn't it?'

Yes, agreed Greg, that was the way the world went.

CHAPTER XV

POSSIBILITIES

There is something in the motion of a train stimulating to sleep or thought. Being disinclined to sleep, Greg sat in the second-class compartment of the train returning him to Manchester, alone apart from a commercial traveller who seemed miraculously disinclined for conversation, and tried to think the case through.

He had now been through, albeit superficially, the Walter Machin papers. So far as he knew, everything that had been transcribed had been lodged with Jackson's, in copy. If that was so, it was difficult to believe that anyone started the fire with a view to destroying some secret in the papers. It was too late for that, and nothing discreditable had leapt out from Greg's perusal. The clue to the crime, if crime there was, must be in the human beings themselves, and in their relationships with each other.

On any reasonable assessment of motive and opportunity, Viola Machin must surely stand high. She had recently quarrelled with Hilda, who was the only person who stood in the way of Viola imposing her own version of people and events on posterity. And to an old person, 'setting the record straight', or straight as they saw it, could be very important. The two of them—as far as was known—were alone in the house. There was also the possibility of sexual jealousy, going way back, but Greg had thought that over a lot, and still did not feel inclined to take the possibility seriously. As far as he could see, Viola Machin's marriage had followed a familiar pattern: begun from sheer sexual passion, aggravated by loneliness and perhaps desertion, it had quickly gone sour; it sounded as if Viola had suffered disillusion and frustration—the sexual side had not proved enough, and other aspirations, social ones perhaps, or aspirations of Walter making a mark in the literary world, had not been fulfilled. This pattern, clear enough at the time, had been obscured by the revival of Walter Machin's reputation, and Viola's desire to rewrite history, to have her marriage accepted as perfect, if tragically brief. But sexual jealousy of an unsatisfactory husband's former wife—this didn't seem likely: Viola's own love-life, Greg guessed, had been varied enough for her to ignore any previous entanglements of her second husband's. Hilda, for her, simply represented another point of view, which she did not want to get a hearing.

About the opportunity, Greg was less than happy: if the fire, designed to cover up the murder (which it so successfully had), was started in the attic, *could* Viola have done it? With difficulty, perhaps—slowly and heavily. But surely it would have been both noisy and dangerous?

The financial motive was looking stronger all the time. Those books represented money—a lot of money. If the agreement between Viola and Hilda was to hold—as apparently it had held after the murder—then Rose was the principal beneficiary. Also interested in Rose's financial position would be her husband and—if his suspicions were correct—Hilary Seymour-Strachey. How much did these people know about the likely profitability of the books? Rose, he had discovered, knew quite a lot—because Hilda had told her. The others, presumably, would have known just as much as she cared to tell them.

Financially, the elder son of Viola, and his wife, seemed the best bet, if character were taken into account, too. They seemed to love money, want it, need it. Yet the fact was, they had *not* benefited by the death, nor would they necessarily do so. Now if it had been Viola that had died . . . An interesting thought . . . If it had been Viola. And then there was another interesting thought: if it had been Viola *as well*. As it very easily might have been. Would Desmond Seymour-Strachey have honoured any agreement his mother had come to with Hilda, would he have considered himself obliged to pay half the royalties to Rose?

Opportunity for these suspects was difficult to determine—so much *more* difficult because this was not an official investigation, and he was not a regular investigator. How *did* one ask someone what they were doing on the night of the twenty-eighth if one was pretending to be engaged in merely casual conversation? Rose, he knew, had had an opportunity—her dog-walking provided her with that. Her absence (if it was regular and fairly lengthy) would presumably have given a similar opportunity to her husband. But as far as the others were concerned he hadn't a clue, and, rack his brains as he might, he had very little idea how he could find out.

For the rest, there were two figures on the margin of the investigation. Kronweiser would most certainly never have burnt the papers, even to cover up murder. But what if he had taken advantage of an accidental blaze to kill Hilda? Perfectly possible, if he was on the spot. But why should he want to? There was no motive, and Greg had no notion whether he was around the house at the time or not. If so, he had certainly been working later than usual.

Just thinking for a moment of character alone: who would he pick as murderer? Mentally he grouped them. Possible murderers: Viola Machin, Desmond Seymour-Strachey, Mr Kronweiser. Unlikely murderers: Rose Clough, Bill Clough. Impossible to say: Margaret, Hilary and Gerald Seymour-Strachey.

Even as he grouped them, he shook his head: what did he really know about these people? Why did he think Rose unlikely? Because she seemed a nice woman and had had a nice mother, with whom she seemed to get on well. It was ludicrously nebulous. In fact he knew nothing of importance about her at all.

And what, then, was there left for him to do? The background, certainly, still needed some filling out. He wanted to finish reading the works of Walter Machin that were available, perhaps have a good look at Gerald Seymour-Strachey's autobiography and other writings, talk to people who knew Machin—grilling senior citizens in pubs, as he put it to himself: filling them with weak beer to stimulate their weaker memories. It was all necessary, no doubt, but with all the optimism of his youth he couldn't see that it looked promising. And after that? Somehow—*somehow*—to find out who was where on the night of Hilda Machin's death.

And suddenly it struck Greg that there was something else of possible interest. There was Walter Machin's will.

Greg had rung Helen from London to tell her when he would be arriving in Manchester, and she had promised to work late and go out with him for a meal. Her office was only ten minutes from Manchester Victoria, and Greg decided to step it out through the grey, grubby streets, in the foggy chill of a May evening.

He was just turning into the featureless modern office block that housed the Heyes-Farringdon Company where Helen worked, when his eye was suddenly
caught by a sign on the other side of the street: The
Olivera Typewriter Company. He stopped in his
tracks, scanned the window opposite for some
minutes, then turned to walk into the building much
more slowly and thoughtfully than before.

'That Olivera office opposite,' he said to Helen as
he walked into the office—'what sort of place is it?'

'That,' said Helen, 'is a fine greeting for a girl.'

'That Olivera office opposite,' said Greg, coming up
to her desk, sitting himself on the edge of it, and kiss-
ing her twice—'what sort of place is it?'

'That,' said Helen, very coolly indeed, '—and I
don't think two very perfunctory kisses make things
very much better—is an office-supply place. You've
heard of Olivera typewriters, for heaven's sake. They
supply those—and filing cabinets and desks and desk
chairs and all that sort of thing. Bulk orders mostly,
to big firms. It's the central Olivera place in Manchester.'

'Not the sort of place you'd go to to pick up a new
ribbon?'

'I shouldn't think so—not unless you wanted a dirty
look from the sales staff.'

'Was that the place you saw Kronweiser going
into?'

'Yes, that's right. I told you.'

'You just said office place. I thought you meant a
kind of stationers'. What could Kronweiser want at a
place like that, do you think?'

'Well, I suppose you *could* go there for a new
typewriter, though as I say, they're mainly interested
in bulk orders. Perhaps they're cheaper here than in
the States.'

'Hmm—well, perhaps. It doesn't sound likely. Kronweiser's gone, I heard the other day. Back home to finish his great work of rehabilitation. I suppose he *could* have had one sent to the plane to get it duty-free. How would I find out?'

'Well,' said Helen, 'I *do* know a girl who works in the outer office there, and we *do* sometimes meet up for lunch and I *could* try to put her on to it. . . . On the other hand, I *am* a girl who likes a bit of old-fashioned interest taken in her, and I *do* get cheesed when I have to take second place, especially when it's to a dead widow of seventy-odd . . .'

For the rest of the evening, Greg showed interest.

'Are you alone?' asked Helen, when she phoned through the next afternoon to the College of Further Education staff common room during Greg's free period.

'No,' said Greg, looking towards an elderly female colleague in a drab woolly frock, hunched over piles of marking but twitching at the ears for anything of scandalous human interest. 'Can I help you at all?'

'Well, I took my friend from Olivera's to lunch, which will cost you a couple of quid or a night out at the weekend. She promised to find out, and she's just come back with the results. Now—he came in there with a letter.'

'I see,' said Greg greyly. 'Was it any particular date?'

'Yes—that was the point. It was dated nineteen thirty-nine, and it was about a visit to London.'

'Ah yes,' said Greg. 'As a matter of fact, I think I may have seen it.'

'Well, he had the original, and he wanted to know if the machine it was typed on was available before nineteen thirty-nine.'

It was with difficulty that Greg restrained himself from saying 'What!', but knowing that his colleague would assume that he was being told he was about to become an unmarried father, and spread it, he said in the same world-weary voice: 'That's very interesting.'

'Well, they investigated, and apparently it was quite easy, because it was a very distinctive typeface, which they'd only used on one machine. He came back a day or two later and they told him it definitely had been available before nineteen thirty-nine.'

'*Had?*'

'Yes. The machine was only on sale between nineteen thirty-six and nineteen forty. He seemed satisfied, said he was grateful, and it was what he had hoped.'

'I see,' said Greg. Then, unable to frame any neutral question to follow up, he just said, 'Thank you for the information, hope to see you soon,' and put down the phone.

For the rest of his duty period he walked around in a daze. The information, at first, had seemed to open up new vistas. Mr Kronweiser had been on to something. He had suspected someone of forging letters from Walter Machin. Was that it? Who then? Hilda Machin, presumably. Or perhaps the two old dears together. To keep his interest up. But it sounded more like Hilda alone—it was just the sort of thing to appeal to Hilda's sense of humour. To feed Mr Kronweiser false letters and die of laughter as he lapped them up. Probably she had some old typing paper of Walter's still around in the attic, so she could make them look convincing. It was just like Hilda—and she could tell herself she was giving the Walter Machin industry a boost while she was enjoying a good laugh. Kronweiser had got on to it and—what? Killed her? No, that was nonsense. Not just because it was a ridiculously inadequate motive, but because it wasn't true. The typewriter wasn't a later model than 'thirty-nine. Kronweiser *hadn't* proved forgery.

Then—what? It was a dead end. For Kronweiser as for him. Kronweiser's suspicions were set at rest, and he had gone back to the States. As for Greg—he was precisely where he had been before.

Or was he missing the point? Was that *not* the reason behind Kronweiser's enquiry at Olivera's? And if it was not, what in the wide world was it?

He racked his brains till he finished teaching, and he racked them while he tried to sleep, but nothing presented itself. He had a dreadful feeling that the next step would have to be the old-age pensioners.

CHAPTER XVI

CONVERSATION PIECE

The Hamley Arms, Oswaldston, 30 May.
'Oh aye, she were a gradely lass, were our 'Ilda. Thanks a lot—good pint this. Aye, a real bobby-dazzler. Born just round t'corner from us, so we felt right proud of her. Good with the kids at school, too. There were many as reckoned she threw 'erself away when she started going wi' Walter Machin.'

'Why was that? He was in a good job, wasn't he? And he seems to have kept in work.'

'Oh aye—he were foreman, or a bit later on he were, any road. Youngest works foreman there's been around these parts. Still, when all's said, it's not a clean job. There's many thought our 'Ilda, being a school teacher, ought to have aimed higher. Gone for something with a bit of class. She had the looks for it, too.'

'Did she have any other boy-friends?'

'There was plenty as was willing, any road. Headmaster for one, only he were married. But no—Walter it had to be. An' then, within a few years, they'd got the babby an' she'd given up teaching. What a waste! Our Bill were in 'er class, an' he were that upset. Not that she were soft wi' them—firm but fair, that was our 'Ilda.'

'Do you think it was a happy marriage—at first, I mean?'

'Depends on how you look at it, doesn't it? Depends what she expected out of it.'

'What do you mean?'

'Well, like, did she go into it with her eyes shut or open? Because I mind our Dad saying: "She'd do better to take on a class o' twelve-year-olds than take on Walter Machin!" An' he were right, because he were a bit of a lad.'

'He had an eye for the women, you mean?'

'Oh aye. Always had, from when he were a lad. Damn near had to get married while he were still apprentice. Mind you, fair's fair: they went after him just as much as he went after them—he were a good-looking chap, well set-up, like. And of course wi' him working in a mill, there wasn't any shortage of volunteers. I remember one time—before he met Hilda—he seemed to have a different lass every Saturday night for a year or more. And he didn't have to stand them pictures, either! Hilda must have known all about it, so it just depends on whether she thought she could reform him, or whether she were content to take him as he was.'

'Because he didn't change after they married?'

'I wouldn't say that. Let's say he cut down by eighty per cent. I suppose you ought to call that reform, in any language, eh? Good beer this, lad . . .'

The Dog and Whistle, Bury, 1 June.
'Oh aye, we were at school together. Proper little rogue and vagabond, was our Walter. Teacher never had a moment's peace with him, and I couldn't count the number of times I've seen him waiting outside the headmaster's study. Always up to some mischief or other. Kept us in stitches.'

'You wouldn't have expected him to become a writer?'

'Writer? Writer! It was all he could do to spell his

own name. Oh no—he never had no time for learnin', not then. He was what you'd call a late developer. Or what's that word that Lizzie—'er as married my grand-son—'as picked up? Under-achiever. She's got one like young Walter Machin, and that's what the headmas-ter said he was. Our Lizzie goes round to everybody and says: "My Stanley's an under-achiever," like it was the Queen's Award to Industry. Pleased as Punch she is. I said to her, I said: "In my time they called it idleness," I said, "if it wasn't stupidity." But she just looks at me pityingly, like I was behind the times and needed to catch up with the latest ideas.'

'What do you think it was in Walter Machin's case?'

'Well, stands to reason he was just lazy, doesn't it? After all, he came to write those books the papers go on about. Must have been a clever enough chap un-derneath. In fact, we all knew he was sharp, sharp as a carving knife. And I know he went to classes and things after he left school. But what he was really good at was machines. By gum, he could make them go! He loved anything mechanical, did Walter. If it was something he hadn't seen before, he'd bend over it like it was a babby, and in half an hour he'd know that machine inside out.'

'Is that why he was made a foreman, do you think?'

'Aye. Firms appreciate that sort of thing. And it was all pure pleasure to Walter. If you asked him what he'd rather have—a night wi' a pretty lass or a day wi' a Rolls-Royce engine, I think he'd have had to toss for it. You could almost hear him purring when he got near anything wi' cogs and pistons.'

'Someone in one of those Sunday newspapers' arti-cles called him "the poet of machinery".'

'Aye, well, I can well believe it. There wasn't much Walter didn't know about machines, and what he didn't know he could learn in five minutes. So it didn't

make a scrap of difference, him being backward, like.
He was always in work, right from the day he left
school.'

'What about his home background?'

'Ee—well, it's getting near my time for going home,
I think I'd better be making a move. . . .'

'Won't you have another drink?'

'Well, I'll just 'ave a quick one—thanks very much.'

The Castle, Blackburn, 2 June.
'Oh aye, he was the light of my life one time, was
Walter Machin. Me and a couple of hundred others.
I used to watch his every movement when he went
around the mill—all the girls did. Wonder we didn't
do ourselves an injury, he was that much of an industrial hazard.'

'What was so special?'

'You wouldn't understand, lad. You're a man—and
the wrong generation an' all. If he appeared in that
door now, probably none of the girls here would give
him a second glance: it's all long hair and round
shoulders now, isn't it, like yesterday's flowers. But
Walter Machin was just what we went for in those
days: we were all daft about him—couldn't think o'
anything else, from morn to night.'

'And I suppose he liked that?'

'Aye, he did. Not that he ever acted cock o' the
walk—ee, doesn't that sound awful? But what I mean
is, he didn't have that high an opinion of himself,
just because he knew he could have any one of us for
the asking. He had a sense of humour, did Walter, so
it never got out of proportion.'

'Did he—well, did he take advantage of the situation?'

'Well, that's one way of putting it. Not how I'd
describe it myself. Because he never got a lass into
trouble—except once, and that was when he was just

a lad. He was very considerate like that—and he taught us girls a thing or two we lived to be grateful for later on, I can tell you.'

'Did you and he—go together?'

'Aye, we did. And for an admission like that from an old woman you can buy me another drink, young man. . . . Ta. Yes, we "went together" for three weeks. It was lovely. Just heaven. I wouldn't like to tell you how often I've thought back on it. Must be hundreds of thousands of times. Because a husband's not the same, is it? At least, mine wasn't.'

'Did you and Walter quarrel?'

'Quarrel? Ee, no, lad: you couldn't quarrel with Walter. You knew from the beginning the terms of the thing, and if you tried to make it more serious than that, you only lost him the quicker. No, there was no quarrel: he just went on to someone else, like he always did. Of course, I'd dreamed my dreams, but I wasn't surprised. I'd known it would happen, all along. I was quite pretty, a neat enough lass, but I wasn't anything special.'

'I suppose Hilda Machin was, then?'

' 'Course she was. She'd had an education, hadn't she? Gone to some sort of college. She could have had her pick, that one. Even then, they was very coy, them two.'

'Coy?'

'He didn't like to admit he'd got hooked—not after the way he'd been going on. That sort's always the most embarrassed, aren't they? And she'd got modern ideas, and all—about married women being slaves, and what not—though to my way of thinking it's always a toss-up which is the slave. Any road, they crept off to Bury one weekend—it was where his mam lived, where he'd been brought up and gone to school. And they got it done at the Registry, very quiet. There's still folk around here will tell you they never were married at all, but it's a lie: my Aunt Florrie was char at Registry Office, and she saw them there.'

'Did he change after he got married?'

'Well, all men do don't they?'

'He gave up chasing the girls, did he?'

'Oh—he didn't lose his eye, not Walter. But he did cut down—it was only now and then. You'd know when he was breaking loose: you'd see him walking round t'mill like a cat wi' two tails, and you'd say to yourself—"There's something on." O' course, I only knew him a few years after he got married. I moved here to Blackburn wi' my Arthur in 'thirty-seven, and I never saw him again to my knowledge. But he was no age when he died, and if you ask me it was probably like that to the end, knowing Walter.'

'He wasn't the faithful type?'

'Well—he was and he wasn't. I think there was really only one woman for him after he married. He was faithful to her—but not *strictly* faithful, if you get my meaning.'

'I get your meaning.'

The Pendle Arms, Oswaldston, 5 June.

'Well, I never knew him really, till right at the end. I mean, I did get work at his mill in the summer of 'forty—I'd been on t'dole for four years, since I left school—but he went into the RAF not long after, and I didn't see him again till late 'forty-six. He wasn't the same chap, I'll tell you that. I knew him well enough to spot *that*. Perhaps he was sick then—I don't know. It was only two years or so later that he died—TB or summat. But he wasn't the same chap.'

'Less lively?'

'Aye—much more thoughtful, brooding like. Hardly ever cracked a joke, and if he did it was bitter, like as not. O' course I don't want to exaggerate: now and then you'd get sparks out of him—he'd tell a good

story, he'd chat up one o' the lasses, or go to t'pub wi'
the lads. But it wasn't often. He hadn't the heart, like
he had before.'

'What do you think it was changed him?'

''Appen it was t'war, 'appen it was his marriage
breaking up, 'appen it was this new wife. That's what
most put it down to. Aye, I'll have another, if you're
ordering. . . . Ta. Yes, he used to make some
pretty nasty remarks about wives and nagging, did
Walter, after he came back.'

'He was still foreman, wasn't he?'

'Oh aye. But he wasn't a good one. Not that he
wasn't a marvel with machinery, a real wizard—aye,
he was still that. But he couldn't organize people any-
more. He forgot things, forgot faces, nothing really
ran like it should. It was like he had something on
his mind the whole time.'

'Perhaps he was thinking of his writing?'

'Well, he shouldn't have been, should he—not in
firm's time? Any road, he wasn't writing. Some o' the
chaps'd ask him, joking like, and he'd say: "I've given
that there up. The depression's gone out of fashion."
I don't think he ever set great store by it.'

'What makes you say that?'

'Well, there was one chap there was a reading type
o' chap—got into Parliament later, the ambitious
type, you know—and he'd say: "What did you say this
or this for, Walter, in *The Factory Whistle?* You
know that's wrong. You know that's not how a lathe
works." An' 'e'd say: "Them books isn't for the likes
o' you, Jack. They're for folks down South, who don't
know a lathe from a loom." No, he were never puffed
up about his writing, wasn't Walter.'

'You say he talked about his home life sometimes?'

'Oh aye, off and on. Everybody does, some time or
other, over a pint.'

'Do you think he was happy?'

'I know damn well he wasn't—whatever that toffee-nosed bitch his wife may say now. From what he let drop I'd say she was on at him morning, noon and night. I reckon he was trapped at last, like a good many others.'

'Trapped? How could she have trapped him?'

'I reckon she told him the youngest boy was his—worked on him that way. Because he was soft underneath, was Walter. Perhaps she knew he wanted a son, perhaps she said her first marriage broke up because her first husband found out he wasn't the father.'

'Why do you think that?'

'Well, there must have been something of that sort. Because I mind one night, just a few weeks before he left t'mill for good—and by gum he looked sick then, more like a shadow than the man he was before the war—well, we were all out wi' a lad as was getting married in a rush, you know. And Walter, he looked in his glass, all evening, proper gloomy-like. And just before he went, he said: "Funny," he said. "I nearly got caught like that, when *I* was seventeen. And to think I was such a fool as to let it happen when I was thirty-five!" '

The Railway Hotel, Oswaldston, 6 June.
'Yes, he was my patient. Really sad case, that, because he'd been a fine man. They should never have let him into the RAF—can't think why they didn't spot it. Anyway, his years there can't have done him any good.'

'There was no hope of saving him?'

'Not by the time I saw him. If we could have got him to a warm climate we might have kept him alive for a year or two more than we did. But that was 'forty-seven: you know how difficult travel was then. And there was no money to send him. Anyway, I don't think the chap *wanted* to live.'

'You mean he wouldn't have liked to be an invalid—having been so healthy all his life?'

'That, partly. He had no resources. He fretted in bed—he was used to doing things, living a practical life. But then, I don't think he was happy anyway. "Do your worst, Doc," he'd say: "Put an end to it. There's nothing coming to me that'll be worse than her yak-yakking all day." Shouldn't tell you this, but when you're retired there's nothing much they can do to you, is there? No, I'd say that wife of his was as unsuitable a sick-nurse as you could find.'

'So he hadn't much fight in him?'

'Not an ounce. Just waiting for the end. You know, he sent me with a message to his first wife before he died. I didn't like doing it—seemed a bit hole-in-the-corner, you know—but he said if I didn't take it, no one would.'

'What was it?'

'He just said: "Tell her: 'You always did say I did daft things if you weren't around to stop me.'" It wasn't very romantic, but you know, when I told her, she cried her heart out. I say, will you have another beer?'

'Thanks,' said Greg.

CHAPTER XVII

HAPPY FAMILIES

After Walter Machin's last doctor had left the Railway Hotel, Greg remained on his stool by the bar, sunk in thought. He had heard (and drunk) so much in the last few days that his mind was a haze of impressions and conjectures which refused to sort themselves out or lead in any one direction. And he was tormented by the idea, by the conviction, that he had missed something. Somewhere, he told himself, somewhere there had been an indication—what was it? A contradiction, an unlikelihood, a piece of the jigsaw which glared out with a contrasting colour nowhere else evident in the picture. *Something*, in one of these conversations over the last few nights, had gone past him, and the momentary uneasiness it aroused had been forgotten. How was it to be dredged up again?

Greg remained perched uneasily, staring down into his glass, feeling like a juggler who suddenly finds he is keeping eleven balls in the air instead of ten, and wonders where on earth the other ball has come from.

'Oh, hello,' said a voice brightly. 'I thought teachers didn't go drinking in pubs.'

'You're way out of date,' said Greg automatically; 'nowadays we do nothing else.' He turned to see the plain little face of Margaret Seymour-Strachey, sur-

mounted by a fawn, church-going hat of the dreariest
kind. She had clearly been out for the evening.

'What will you—?'

'No, no,' she said, with something like a simper. 'I
have horribly expensive tastes.' Horrible, anyway. She
ordered a snowball, and fumbled in her bag for the
price of it. The movements of her hands were quick,
nervous, not well controlled, and she dropped a five-
pence piece on the floor. 'I'm just glad to see a face I
know,' she said when she had retrieved it. 'I'm not
used to coming into a pub on my own. We married
women have it so *good*, really, if we only realized it!'

'Shall we move over there?' suggested Greg, nodding to a vacant corner and hoping his intentions
were not mistaken: he aimed at cosy conversation
rather than anything intimate. The speed with which
Margaret Seymour-Strachey accepted his offer suggested she was desperate for someone to talk to.

'*Could* we, do you think?' she said. 'It is awfully
bright here, isn't it?'

When they had settled themselves in their corner,
she showed every indication of making the conversa-
tional running: she was chirpy, sparkling—almost too
much so, as if tensed up.

'I felt I *had* to come in and have a drink, because I
did need one so. Isn't it awful? I've been to the Blackburn Literary Club—such an interesting talk, but very
high-powered. It was on Harrison Ainsworth and *The
Lancashire Witches*. I do get rather fed up with *The
Lancashire Witches* and *Mist Over Pendle,* but there
you are. I wasn't going to go, but . . .' She subsided into silence over her snowball. To Greg she
didn't seem to be making much sense—saying whatever came first into her head and contradicting herself. Maybe behind the gush there was something she
wanted to say but wasn't brazen enough to bring out

too openly. Into the pause he slipped a tentative completion of her sentence:

'But you felt you had to get out?'

She shot him a sharp little gaze—as if unsure as yet whether he was friend or foe. But seeing a look of sympathy, she replied: 'Yes, that's right. Being in the house was beginning to seem like being in Broadmoor, you know? But there—I don't want to burden you with my troubles.'

'Oh, not at all,' said Greg guilelessly. 'I realize Mrs Machin can be difficult.'

'Difficult! She can be bloody impossible!' The words had come out with a distinct tang of broad Lancashire, but she immediately withdrew into her pseudo-Southern gentility. 'But there, I know what a friend you are to Mother.'

'Hilda, really,' said Greg. 'I only got to know your mother-in-law through visiting at the house.'

'Oh, is that so? Mother always emphasizes what a *special* friend you were to her too. But perhaps that's one of her ways of annoying me. She almost seems to want to suggest that . . .' She stopped in embarrassment.

'That she has a handsome lover fifty years her junior?' suggested Greg.

'Well, yes, actually. Not that I ever believed her— not for a moment. Of course I know why she says things like that: it's to make me feel bourgeois, provincial, conventional, inhibited—the complete little woman! That's why she cuddles my children the whole time—she's trying to say I lack warmth.' Her face flushed with anger. 'Well, if that's where warmth gets you—a lonely old age, with your only pleasure making trouble for other people—then I'm glad I'm cold!'

Greg felt suddenly sorry for her: she had none of the confidence of Hilda Machin in repelling the sort

of attacks Viola was so expert at mounting. 'Don't
you think,' he said, 'you're reacting in just the way
she wants?'

'Yes, I am, I know, and I can't stop myself! My
God, what sort of life must her husbands have had?'

'Not too good, I've heard,' said Greg, not adding
that he had just been grilling the doctor who signed
her second husband's death certificate. 'You realize
she's trying to be unbearable so that your husband
sees they get a move on with her house?'

'Did she tell you that? How rotten of her to spread
the family troubles all round the town. Not of course
that you would . . .' She subsided into silence at
her tactlessness, and then something like a sob es-
caped her. 'Well, she's certainly succeeding, if that's
what she wants. She should be able to move in by the
end of next week, and I'll never be so happy as when
I wave her goodbye at the front door. I have been on
at Desmond about it, as a matter of fact, which I suppose is what she wanted. My husband has plenty of
influence when he cares to use it,' she concluded with
naive pride.

'He's in insurance, isn't he?'

'That's right. He has a wonderful head for
business. They think the world of him at the
Northern. But nobody seems to value a good business
brain these days, do they? That's why the country's in
such a mess, that's what I always say.'

Once more Margaret Seymour-Strachey's words
seemed to come from the front of her head, and to be
as contradictory as words usually are when they don't
represent what one is really thinking about. What
really was her husband's reputation with the
Northern, Greg wondered? Margaret-Strachey's mouth
was now working convulsively, and her eyes becoming
distinctly swimmy.

'So she's been doing it to hurry things on, has she?

I half suspected it, but I wasn't sure.' Suddenly the
words rushed out in a jumble of grievance and anger.
'She's always behaved like a—like a pig to me. Do you
know she said she wasn't coming to our wedding right
up to the last moment, and when she did consent to
come she behaved as if all the guests on my side were
mud beneath her feet, though our family's always
been very well thought of around here, as I'm sure
you know, and my father could have bought her up a
hundred times and not noticed the difference, and
what was *her* father in New Zealand I wonder, some
sheep dipper or other I wouldn't mind betting—you
know the type that went to the colonies then—or perhaps he was a convict!'

She finished breathlessly, and Greg refrained from
enlightening her on the history of New Zealand. She
took another sip of her drink, and (her mouth still
working convulsively) she went on.

'You know, I gave her that room to herself when
she came to us, because I thought it would be better,
and she treated me like a servant—well, you saw,
didn't you?—and when she'd got all the fun and sense
of power out of *that* little game she started coming
down with us. Said she wanted to watch television,
though she *didn't* watch—just sat there making sarcas-
tic remarks or calling the children to her and giving
them sweets and kisses—it's disgusting. I said, "For
God's sake, Desmond, hire her a television," but he
said no because we're *not* well off, not well off at all,
and we're having to *keep* her, she hasn't offered a
penny, not that we'd accept of course, and anyway
Desmond said there wasn't any point because if we
got her a television she'd think of something else,
want to play cards or something, and that would be
worse—and he's right, it would, because a game of
bridge with her is like the cold war all over again.'

She subsided and looked around the bar to see if

she was making an exhibition of herself. Seeing everyone engaged in their own private confessionals, she
sipped her drink with renewed confidence.

'So she's been coming down with you, has she?'
asked Greg.

'That's right. Then last night she said she wouldn't
come tonight because there was nothing on—she'd
have a quiet night in her room. So I decided not to
go to the Literary Club but to stay at home. But she
must have heard me say so, because at seven she came
down and said she'd overlooked this *marvellous*
Stockhausen concert on Two—well, I just put on my
coat and flung out of the house. . . . And I'm *not*
going back until television's over!'

Her eyes were now full of tears of rage or self-pity,
and she turned and fumbled in her bag. '*Would* you
get me another?' she asked Greg, handing him a
pound note.

When Greg returned with the snowball, Margaret
Seymour-Strachey had shifted her position so as to be
better shielded from the rest of the Saloon Bar, and it
was clear that she had not managed to get control
over herself, for she was now sobbing away quietly.

'Thank you,' she said. 'You're very kind. I don't
know *why* I should burden you with this and make
an exhibition of myself in front of everyone.' A
louder sob broke out. 'But I can't help it! I just can't
bear to go home! My own home, and I love it, and I
just can't face it! I've had three weeks of being ordered about, laughed at, sneered at, talked over the
head of, ignored. And I *can't* stand any more of it!
I'm not strong. I've never been strong. Do you think
I'm having a nervous breakdown?'

'I'm sure it isn't as bad as that,' said Greg, who
wasn't—who was, in fact, marvelling at the effect of
three weeks of Viola, and wondering whether there
couldn't be more to it than just that. 'Still, couldn't

you get away from it for the next week or so—till she's gone back?'

'If only I could,' sighed Margaret Seymour-Strachey. 'Take the children and get right away.'

'Why shouldn't you? It sounds as if she could cope all right on her own.'

'Oh, she could cope. But where could we go?'

'Down to London—or the sea. It's not the season yet. Stay at a hotel.'

'But that costs *money*. Do you *know* what hotels cost these days? We don't *have* that sort of money to throw around. We're really quite modestly off.'

The dreadful genteelism for 'hard up' seemed to be wrung out of her. 'Your family then,' suggested Greg gently.

'But they live here, in Oswaldston. If I took the children there it would be a real breach. Right out in the open. And that's what Desmond absolutely doesn't want because—well, because he's her son, and so on.'

'Haven't you got some old aunt who could be suddenly ill and need you?'

'No, I haven't really. Anyway, if she were so ill it would look funny taking the children—and I'm *not* leaving them with her!' For a moment her pale, uninteresting face lighted up with spite. 'She's so *sexual*, don't you think? Do you know, she's got the idea that her first husband would like to marry her again!'

'What!' said Greg. So Gerald's girl-friend had been right! An undue pressure of interest had come into his tone (almost as if he were interested in the position himself), but Mrs Seymour-Strachey did not notice. Greg leaned forward conspiratorially, as if one touch of malice made the whole world kin. She went on: 'But it's funny too, isn't it? She's convinced he's just waiting for a sign to pop over and propose!'

'What makes her think that?'

'Desmond told her his father suggested a meeting, and that's what she read into it. It's pathetic really.'

'You don't think she could be right?'

'Oh, I don't think so. Desmond says it was the woman he lives with—isn't it awful, at his age!—who *really* suggested there should be a get-together. Though he says he's always very *interested* in her, and asks about her a lot. But I don't think he would be so *stupid!*' She giggled. ' "Once more into the breach, dear friends." '

'He could be interested in her money.'

'It would have to be that, wouldn't it?' Her eyes narrowed. 'If it were true, she'd have to be *protected* against someone like that, wouldn't she?'

Greg offered to see Margaret Seymour-Strachey home, but she said she was *much* better now, and it was *such* a relief to get things off her chest like that. 'And I'm not sure Desmond would like it if he saw us,' she added with another little giggle. 'And heaven *knows* what Mother would say if she saw!' She raised her chin a little, and a hard look came into her eyes. 'If she's downstairs when I get home, I'm going *straight* up to my bedroom!'

When he got home to his flat, Greg did not go straight into his bedroom. He switched on a few lights, took off his coat and tie and rolled up his sleeves, then he pottered around the kitchen making himself a good-night mug of milkless tea. The quiet, tedious activity helped to get some of his chaotic impressions from the evening into some sort of order. Then he walked around the little living-room, cradling the mug in his hands, and thinking. After a time he switched on the television. Some royal anniversary, death, separation or divorce was being made the excuse to trot out a lot of cheap old newsreel footage, but it didn't matter what was on. Greg

was of the generation which found television very
good to think during, and he let his mind range
freely over what he had recently learned.

Money still seemed to be at the forefront. There
were no prizes for guessing, after tonight, that the
Desmond Seymour-Stracheys were living on a financial knife-edge, and would be interested in any sudden accession of wealth, by any means, from any
source. But then money, or *some*thing, seemed suddenly to have brought Gerald Seymour-Strachey from
the hazy background to the centre of the picture. He
remembered the woman he lived with saying 'she's the
only woman in the world for him'. And now he had
found that Viola was convinced he was itching to propose again. Was this just because she saw herself as a
Frieda Lawrence figure, or was there some firmer
basis for it? And was the basis love (in one of its
many varieties) or money? She had made her second
husband's life a hell, it seemed. Had her first husband
had it any better? Why should Shadrach contemplate
for a moment stepping back into the burning fiery
furnace?

'With the unexpected accession of their parents to
the throne,' said the voice from the television, with
that odd blend of reverence and condescension
reserved for royalty and its doings, 'the little
princesses had to reconcile themselves to seeing less
and less of their mother and father. In April nineteen
thirty-nine they went to the quay at Southampton to
see them off on a three months' visit to the United
States and Canada . . .'

Two rather pudding-faced little girls in a limousine
were succeeded on the screen by a smiling George VI
and Roosevelt, with wives, at the Roosevelt country
estate. Greg tried to switch his mind back to the problem in hand.

Gerald Seymour-Strachey's name coming to the

forefront of the picture so unexpectedly made it
worth looking more closely at him—in the past as well
as the present. Had he really moved out before the
Viola-Machin romance got going? *Had* he ditched Viola, as he said, or was it *vice versa*? Had he, perhaps,
put up a fight? Greg had managed to get all his major books from the library, so they could conceivably
help . . .

'*Three* months' trip to the United States and
Canada . . . *Three* months' trip to the United
States and Canada . . .

The words from the television set pounded re-
lentlessly to the front of his mind. 'In *April* nineteen
thirty-nine . . . for a *three* months' visit . . .'

And yet—and *yet.* There was that letter from Walter in the archive at Jackson's, dated 2 June 1939.
'The King and Queen went by. What guys!'

They could not have driven by. They were in
America. The letter was a fake. Kronweiser had been
right after all.

One up for American scholarship.

CHAPTER XVIII

HALF LIGHT

When he woke from an exhausted sleep Greg had—he felt—one piece of the jigsaw definitively in place: the letter from Walter Machin to Hilda dated 2 June 1939 was a fake.

Of *course* there were other possible interpretations: that Walter Machin did not recognize his sovereign; that the people who swept by him in a limousine through Admiralty Arch were no higher in the scale than some uppity Tory MP and his lady wife. But *no*. That sort of mistake was almost inconceivable, in an age of mass communications.

The next step forward would seem to be: that the letter had been forged by Hilda Machin. The transcript had been labelled by Kronweiser, 'Given me by Mrs Hilda Machin, 21 April 1978.' Hilda, then, had been forging letters from her late husband. No doubt she had felt safe: probably she still had his old typewriter, not greatly used since the separation. Probably she had found a sufficient stock of unused paper in the attic—yellowed enough with age to carry conviction. She had thought it a foolproof notion, but had slipped up on detail, like so many.

Why had she done it? Greg thought back on the Hilda he had known with a surge of affection: he could almost see her, chuckling over the typewriter as she composed the letter. Or perhaps her whole being had been flooded with the personality of the real, dead Walter, as she tried to reproduce his style, the dash of his personality, his iconoclastic irreverence. Surely she had been enjoying herself. Surely it had been a joke, prompted by the dreadful heavy seriousness of Dwight Kronweiser and the overreverent attitude to Walter taken up for public reasons by Viola. It had been an attempt to let in a bit of fresh air on the subject.

But perhaps the joke had had a serious point to it too, or at any rate a serious side-effect: it had enabled Hilda to get her side of the story over to posterity. By forging letters from Walter she, paradoxically, felt she could convey a real image of him to stand against the false one. It was one way of having her say.

And the step after that in the deductive process? Who would object to Hilda's little game? Well, Kronweiser, certainly, from a scholarly point of view. But then he had only to ignore the products of Hilda's ingenuity. But what if he had voiced his suspicions to Viola? . . . Greg's mind played on Viola's concern with keeping the record 'straight', meaning that it must tell only her version. He remembered the anguish in her voice as she cried: 'I wonder what she is saying about me!' He remembered the row on the day the newspaper interview had come out—so violent as to be heard from the street. . . . If Mr Kronweiser had confided his suspicions that Hilda was forging letters, what would Viola's reactions have been?

He registered in his mind one other possibility: that the letters had been forged by Kronweiser himself, to fill out the picture of Walter Machin for his book. He furrowed his brow. Would he have had the inventive capacity, the command of idiom? And why that trip to Olivera's? But he docketed the possibility in the filing cabinet of his mind. Then he went and had a vigorous shower.

The vigorous shower did not have any of the bene-
ficial effects such things were generally said to have by
public-school games-masters of a previous age. As he
rather gloomily put together a breakfast of poached
egg and grilled bacon he felt neither particularly
healthy nor particularly clear-minded. He was like a
man who has made one step forward into unknown
territory and stands looking for a path. If only the
will had come. He had sent for a copy, but the bu-
reaucratic machine seemed to be taking its time. Still,
he had until two o'clock before he had to go into the
College—today was the day he did evening teaching.
He shoved his plates into the sink and took his tea
into the living-room. There, by the easy chair, he had
placed the works of Gerald Seymour-Strachey—three
fairly substantial—looking volumes. With a sigh, and
a glance of regret at the clear, bright day outside, he
settled down in his chair and took up the first of the
tomes.

The autobiography—*Sins of My Old Age and Earlier*—he had already dipped into, and he went back to
it reluctantly for a more systematic reading. The story
it had to tell was interesting enough: childhood and
adolescence in New Zealand, university life in Australia and a stint on the literary pages of the *Sydney
Morning Herald;* arrival in London in the late 'twenties, when the Katherine Mansfield boom was at its
height and there was an unusual keenness to welcome
literary talent from New Zealand; London literary
life in the 'thirties—and so on. What Greg did not
greatly like was the tone. It grated. This was particularly so in connection with the sexual adventures
hinted at in the title—adventures which became a sort
of *leitmotif*, in that the author seemed to feel he had
to have one in every seven or eight pages, preferably
with some piquant variation. It was rather pathetic,
like an ageing colonel looking back on the days of

Empire. And they were narrated with a snickering self-satisfaction, a dated coyness, which Greg found unappetizing. After his sexual initiation by a barmaid in an outback pub, while his father was drinking downstairs (at an age which would seem to be about twelve and a half—but Greg felt the incident had been brought forward significantly, from a feeling that the narrative pace of the opening pages was already flagging), Gerald Seymour-Strachey went on to a variety of girls (occasionally called 'girlies') and later women. Most of them were accorded pseudonyms ('I will call her Sylvia') and given a few lines of narrative, where their function was little more than to illustrate our hero's appetite and prowess.

His marriage was treated very briefly; he recorded it as taking place in 1934, and the bride as being 'at that time newly arrived from New Zealand and as a writer considered highly promising—alas, of how many has this been said!' Her name came up now and again in succeeding chapters, though she was not allowed to have played a significant part in his life. The break-up of the marriage was recorded as taking place in 1943, 'due to the pressures and uncertainties of war'—as if Gerald had been at the very least a fighter ace or undercover agent. The next chapter, however, had him going to Grimsby University, 'to keep the torch of literature alive in a dark period'.

Putting aside the book after an hour or more of solid dipping, Greg decided that Gerald Seymour-Strachey was one of those people who are quite unable to hide the less attractive sides of their personalities from outsiders because these are precisely the sides they themselves are most pleased with. Perhaps this was something he had in common with his elder son.

The major critical work revealed a rather different side to Gerald's personality. The title itself was

designed to pull you up short: *The Heterosexual
Strain in Modern English Literature*. Greg had first
read it as 'Homosexual', and that of course was the
joke. Heterosexuality among English writers, it was
being implied, was so much the exception to the rule
as to demand special treatment. The whole of the in-
troduction was a solemnly tongue-in-cheek exposition
of this notion, though Greg had the impression that
later the joke rather ran out of steam (as the book
very nearly did run out of authors to treat) .

The Ern Malley Affair, a slimmer volume, was an
examination of a famous Australian literary hoax of
the mid-'forties, in which bogus poems of impenetra-
ble obscurity were foisted on a literary magazine. It
was not clear why the matter deserved a book to itself.

Putting the volumes aside, Greg tried to consider
the personality they evoked as a whole. They were
rather unpleasantly self-satisfied for a start—and this
was not incompatible with the impression made on
him by the man himself at their meeting. These
books were also very dated, in that they were *jokey*—
look at me being clever, they seemed too often to be
crying. And nothing dates more easily than the clever
wheezes of a previous generation. It was rather as if
the author—for all the breadth of his experience
which he was constantly insisting upon—had never
quite grown up. All in all, this was a man who delighted in proving how clever he was—and sometimes,
as a corollary, in suggesting how dim and credulous
other people were.

He let his mind play over the man as he had felt
him at their meeting, as he now knew him from his
books: vain, opinionated, hearty, jokey. Why, he
though idly, *why* had Walter Machin not appeared in
the volume of autobiography? Gerald Seymour-
Strachey had *not* explained that satisfactorily at their

meeting. On the one hand he had said that he was forgotten, so why mention him? On the other, that he was not forgotten—that there were pockets of admirers who still cherished his books throughout the long years when they were out of print. He couldn't have it both ways. And as far as Greg could judge there were a great many writers who had found a place in the book who were quite as obscure or more so—poets whose flame had died with the end of the war, one-off playwrights whose experimental verse dramas had caused no more than a ripple of interest even in their own time.

Why then omit to mention Walter? Surely the reason must lie in the ridiculous sexual vanity of the man: he had left him out to pay him back, posthumously, for stealing his wife. To mention him would be to revive an old humiliation. Otherwise, if place could have been found for these minor poets and playwrights, not to mention jumped-up journalists who also figured all too prominently, surely a few sentences could have been spared for the man he himself had described as the one working-class writer who remained working-class—the man whom the *Sentinel* had called 'the poet of work'.

The phrase stirred a vague uneasiness in his mind. 'The Poet of Work'. It sounded good. And yet, and yet . . . The man in the pub who remembered one of his workmates complaining to Walter that he had got the details of the factory machinery wrong . . . Mr Causeley at Jackson's saying in his superior Southern style that people had written complaining that Machin had said 'bobbin-waggler' when he should have siad 'throcket-shuttle'. He was flim-flamming, of course, but that must have been the general burden of the letters.

But Walter Machin should not have got the mechanical details wrong.

There were the other readers, of course. The man
on the train, the teacher who had been in Lancashire
for three years, but felt he never really knew it until
Walter Machin revealed it to him. There were the
critics on the newspapers who had praised the vividness and accuracy of the books. But when it came
down to it, it was the people who didn't really know
Lancashire who found Walter Machin impressive.
The ones who knew, the men of his own class, the
men who worked in the mills with him, they were
unconvinced. . . .

Ern Malley . . .

His meditations were interrupted by a plop on the
front-door mat. It was the second post. Going absently
to see what it was, Greg found it was from Somerset
House. The photocopy of the will he had requested.
Feverishly opening it, he scanned it through with his
mind in a whirl. Most if it he knew: the copyright on
his works to his wife Viola; the manuscripts to his
former wife Hilda Machin; a small sum of money to
his mother, still alive at the time of the making of the
will. There was nothing out of the ordinary.

But the surprise came at the end. The signature
was not the signature of the letters and contracts he
had seen at Jackson's. The name Walter Machin was
written in a large, rounded, unconnected and uncertain script.

It was the signature of a man who was to all in-
tents and purposes illiterate.

CHAPTER XIX

THE SWORD OF DAMOCLES

Greg Hocking's second trip to Borthwick was under-
taken on one of the most glorious days of the year,
when the dales spread out before his eyes in rolling
profusion, as if they were concerned to proclaim:
there are beauties in England still.

Greg hardly saw them.

He drove, he munched sandwiches prepared by
Helen the night before, and he thought. Round and
round like circus horses went the questions in his
mind: He must have done it surely he must have
done it—but *why?* Is there a link I haven't come
across yet? A link with Viola? An emotional link? Or
is there a financial link? A financial link with Viola?

A quotation came to his mind: 'Who would have
thought the old man to have so much blood in him?'
He amended it to: 'Who would have thought the old
man to have so much spunk in him?'

The guts to commit murder. Could he see Gerald
Seymour-Strachey as a killer? Had he completely
misunderstood him at their first meeting? What was
there that could make that man into a murderer?
Money—at his age? But then, most misers were old.
Vanity—yes, that seemed more likely. Especially sexual vanity. Or to keep his secret? But surely . . .

He pulled up some way from the cottage and left
the car on the outskirts of the village. He was dressed
very inconspicuously in jeans and short-sleeved check

shirt, but he found everyone looked at him, as people in villages will. But he came on the cottage obliquely, and was able to stand for a minute or two in the shadow of a tree, watching the man he had come to see.

The figure wandering through the garden towards the front door of the cottage was not quite as Greg remembered him. For a start, he seemed to be wandering aimlessly, like a dog through a ghost town. At their first interview, Gerald Seymour-Strachey had seemed to be a decided old man, quite confident of himself and his needs. Then, this figure looked as if seediness was beginning to set in: his shoulders drooped, and the bottom button of his jacket was missing. The old Gerald had been as much a model of smartness for the over sixty-fives as his ex-wife.

When Greg touched the latch of the garden gate, Gerald Seymour-Strachey's head spun round hopefully. The expression on his face faded, however, to one of mere polite welcome.

'Oh hello,' he said. 'I thought . . .' Then he came forward and extended his hand. 'Nice of you to come back so soon.'

'I hope it's not inconvenient?'

'No, no, not in the least.' The hands flopped indeterminately, and he looked doubtfully at the front door. 'Only thing is—the house is in a bit of a mess. Do you want to come in?'

'Well, it might be easier,' said Greg. 'I don't worry about mess. I'm a bachelor myself.'

Gerald Seymour-Strachey looked at him hard. 'Just temporarily in my case, you know. The little lady's had to go away for a bit—sick relative—you know how it is.'

'Of course,' said Greg.

They went inside the cottage. So far there were no very obvious signs of Gerald's forlorn status. Things seemed tidy enough to the unpractised eye. Only

through the door of the kitchen could Greg see any
indications that the usual female hand was absent.
There were piles of washing-up, a smell of burnt
food, and plates still on the table.

'Difficult when there's no woman around,' said Gerald. 'Not used to it. Tried to get a woman from the
village, but I couldn't.' A tired imitation of the old
roguishness wafted over his face. 'I suppose I have a
certain reputation . . .'

They went into the study, slightly dusty, but still
immaculately tidy. Gerald offered tea or beer, but
withdrew the first by adding: 'Beer's quicker.' Greg
accepted the beer. He did not want to strain his host's
goodwill from the beginning.

'Thought of a story I didn't tell you last time,' said
Gerald, as he brought the beer in. He settled himself
into his desk chair and launched into an endless story
of cowardice, duplicity and spleen among the minor
luminaries of his set in 'thirties literary London. It
was not edifying, it was not even interesting—and to
add insult to injury Greg had already read the story
in the autobiography. Does he really think I'm interested in these people, he thought to himself? I
certainly didn't give any indication last time. Or is he
just trying to keep me off one particular subject?

'I've read your autobiography,' he said at the end,
to spare himself further re-hashes. 'I think I understand now why you didn't mention Walter Machin.'

'Oh, Walter,' said Gerald Seymour-Strachey, flap-
ping an arm. 'Of course, you're interested in him
because he's becoming the rage. And he was
enormously talented. But there were other fish in the
sea too. Their hour will come. They'll be re-
vived. . . . We were a *wonderfully* promising
generation!'

'I'm sure,' said Greg. 'What I meant, though, about

the difficulty in writing about Walter Machin was—
well, that he was in a sense *two* people, wasn't he?'

Gerald Seymour-Strachey shot a sharp glance at
Greg's ingenuous enquiring face. 'Well, of course, in
a sense that is true,' he said tentatively. 'Yes, he was
complex, definitely complex. I think we mentioned
when you were here last that there was the political
Walter, but also the great life-loving person—always
drinking, and laughing, and womanizing. Yes, it must
seem almost as if there were two different people.'

It was a moderately accomplished performance, but
at the end his voice seemed to fade away into silence
before the polite disbelief he saw etched on Greg's
face.

'I meant,' said Greg, 'that there really were two
Walter Machins, weren't there? The living Walter
Machin, works foreman at Mattingley's, and the writ-
ing Walter Machin . . . And the writing Walter
Machin was you, wasn't it, Professor Seymour-
Strachey?'

Greg was expecting a long silence, or perhaps in-
dignant expostulation, but when he finished speaking
Gerald was looking him straight in the eyes with an
expression not perturbed, or frightened, or cornered,
but simply of amusement, and quite considerable
self-satisfaction.

'Well now,' he said, almost genially, all the tired-
ness and indecision gone, 'I'd like to know how you
work *that* out.'

'Walter Machin was virtually illiterate,' said Greg
confidently. 'I've seen his will, and what his school-
mates say bears it out. I wondered whether Hilda
might have written the books—she certainly wrote
some letters from him, to fool Kronweiser the American researcher. But if she wrote the books, why not
publish them under her own name? Why go through
this whole business of impersonation?'

'Quite, quite,' said Gerald. 'But . . .'

'That applied to absolutely anyone in Walter Machin's usual circle. It seemed to me there were two other possible candidates. There was your ex-wife.'

'Ah yes. Viola. Now why not Viola? Or are you too intimidated to charge her with it?'

'Not exactly. To tell you the truth, I don't think she has the talent.'

Gerald Seymour-Strachey slapped his thigh in high amusement. 'Marvellous. Very sharp, m'boy! I'm sure you'd never dare to tell her *that*, but it's true. The good lady's all performance and no talent.'

'And that left—you.'

'Quite, m'boy, quite. Process of elimination—not the most conclusive of logical processes, though. By the way, no offence—but you never told me what you actually *are*. Are you a research student—a reporter? Eh?'

'Neither,' said Greg. 'But of course there still is the question of *why*.'

'Precisely,' said Gerald, sitting back and to all appearances enjoying himself no end. 'Why should we arrange this rigmarole for the publication of these two books because they were written by me—any more than if they were written by, say, Hilda?'

'Because the whole thing was a hoax—in intention. I think that's in character, isn't it? You like pricking pretensions, you like showing up phonies, you like making a fool of would-be clever people.'

'Well—well—' said Gerald, with a modest twinkle, as if he were being accused of all the cardinal virtues.

'I think in this case you wanted to make a fool of all the big London literary people—the critics, the left-wing writers. They represented the orthodox intellectual opinion of the time. You wanted them to praise this working-class novel to the skies, to say "how marvellously authentic, darling" and all the things they did say at the time, and then show them up. Reveal that the books were sheer fantasy, sheer parody, written by a middle-class colonial who had never been north of the Edgware Road. That's why you were interested in the Ern Malley affair, wasn't it? I've read your book: it was just your sort of hoax—ridiculing intellectual phoniness. They did in nineteen forty-four what you had intended to do in nineteen thirty-nine.'

'Then why was the bubble never pricked in the Walter Machin affair?'

'Because to be a really good hoax the books had to be successful. Otherwise the spoof of the decade was nothing but a squib. The first book was moderately well-received, with your help. But you were writing other stuff—short stories and another novel—and you expected those to do much better. But it didn't work out like that. The war came, and people lost interest in proletarian literature. The whole thing fizzled out and became pointless.' Greg let himself relax back in his seat. 'That's how I reconstruct it.'

Gerald Seymour-Strachey was by now grinning broadly, and there was not a trace of fear or disappointment in his face. He looked like a man who has found that lawyers are trying to trace his whereabouts, and looks forward to a mysterious but exciting surprise.

'Well, well, I'll give it to you, you've done a good job,' he said expansively. 'It's not that I haven't been half expecting something like this to happen. Half hoping for it too, in a way, though it will cut off poor old Viola's new source of income—which is why I've never said anything about it myself since the Machin boom started, of course.'

'You seem pleased.'

'Well, it will be a nine days' wonder, and bags of fun. I must say I was expecting that if anyone got on

to me it was going to be this American Viola has had
working around the place—a typically stupid move on
Viola's part, I may say. Really, the silly woman
deserves to have the whole thing exposed.'

'I must say,' said Greg, 'that the whole affair still
seems pretty fantastic.'

'Fantastic? Not in the least. The truth is always od-
der than fiction—it's only the way people tell it that
makes it sound so dull.'

'I'd like to hear your version of what happened.'

'Oh—it's quite simple, and more or less as you set it
out now. I'd been writing *The Factory Whistle*, and
it was nearly finished. I intended to publish it under
a pseudonym, with a fancy, impeccably proletarian
biography of the author attached. Then we met Walter and Hilda—in the interval of a Noel Coward play,
just as I told you last time—priceless that! We clicked
at once. Then I got this better idea. In the course of
the evening's drinking Walter told us that he was
next thing to illiterate. He could read with some difficulty, but hardly write. He'd been to classes—that's
how he met Hilda—she was teaching them. But Walter was more interested in other things, and he never
learned much, not more than was necessary to him in
his foreman's job. He wasn't stupid, Walter, by a long
chalk, but I suppose you'd have to call him analpha-
betic. Anyway, this seemed to make the joke so much
better.'

'So the thing was agreed then and there, was it?'

'Not exactly. Actually, the next night—' Gerald
looked down embarrassed at his desk—'bit ashamed
about this, actually—that's why I bit your head off last
time. But the next night he came round on his own,
and I went out to the pub for a bottle, and—well—I
knew what Viola wanted, because she made no bones
about it as a rule and it had happened now and then
before. Anyway, I stayed out for an extra ten minutes

or so to give them plenty of time to—see what I mean? Not that they needed extra time, I imagine, knowing both parties. Anyway, I thought it would cement the agreement. And after I got back we sorted the whole thing out over a bottle of Scotch and a couple of pork pies each.'

'How was it done? I suppose you never appeared in the thing at all?'

'No—not at all. I sent the handwritten manuscripts down to Hilda, and she typed them up. The early things were submitted to the publisher handwritten— it seemed to give verisimilitude, somehow, for a writer from the working-class. Later Hilda typed everything including letters to the publisher, and she signed Walter's name. Easy as winking. She'd given up working when the little girl was born, and she was glad of something to do. Of course, Walter was a bit more of a problem sometimes.'

'In what way?'

'Well, for instance, Hilda was supposed to read him over *The Factory Whistle* so he could correct all the technical stuff. It was about factories rather than mills because I didn't know Walter when I wrote it, but he should have known enough to see the details were right. Well, he corrected some things, but I think he dozed off now and again during the reading, because it wasn't his cup of tea. Or perhaps he drank too much stout while he was listening. Anyway the publishers got letters—'

'Yes, so I've heard. Weren't you afraid about the publishers—when he went to meet them, I mean?'

'I was a bit—that they'd give him something for immediate signature or something. But there was nothing to fear. He hammed it up to the skies, had a whale of a time playing the raw North Country lad, and they felt fearfully democratic that they could actually sit down to lunch with him. I only wish I could have been there, but I heard it went off very well, in fact.'

'And you split the money?'

'That's right. Two-thirds to me, one to him—though I think it actually went to Hilda for doing the typing. For the next one I tried to get him to take more—because really he became a kind of collaborator. He was a marvellous story-teller, you know, of the tap-room type. I used to get him to tell me real events—things from his childhood, things about people he knew. Then I'd turn them into short stories. I got the *feel* of what it's like to work with machines from Walter.'

'Didn't that rather blunt the point of the hoax?'

'I suppose it did in a way. We never thought of that, because we enjoyed it so much. I suppose it became more oral literature, really. That story I told you to read—I had it from his own lips! Happened to a mate of his. That's why the stories in *Cotton Town* are so much better than *Factory Whistle,* though nobody realized it at the time. They're authentic. If only the second novel could have come out; it's really very good!'

Gerald Seymour-Strachey looked sideways at Greg, in a wheedling sort of way.

'Why shouldn't the second novel come out?' said Greg slowly.

'Well, I thought naturally, since you're on to the hoax, you'd want to—expose us all.'

'I'm not very interested in the hoax,' said Greg.

Seymour-Strachey stared at him, almost insulted. 'Not interested in the hoax?'

'I'm really only interested in the murder of Hilda Machin,' said Greg.

Greg was expecting Seymour-Strachey to exhibit surprise. Any moderately wary murderer could accomplish that. But what he expressed was surprise com-

bined with a frank, hungry interest. His mouth
sagged open, and his eyes sparkled with an old person's relish for a sensation. It was a totally innocent
reaction.

"*Mur*der?' he said. '*Hil*da? But I'm absolutely *stag*-
gered. 'Nothing's been *said*, has it?'

Greg was momentarily pushed off balance by the
oddity of Gerald's reaction, but before he had time to
gather his forces Gerald's mind was off on a new track
working away with all the added zest of long disuse.

'You said,' he pondered, 'that you weren't a student
and you weren't a reporter. I don't think you're interested in the literary side of this at all. There's something about you . . . I've felt it all along . . . an
air . . . of rectitude, a dreadful uprightness. Are
you trying to play amateur detective, or something?'

Greg's expression gave him away at once.

'Ha! Got it in one! Just like the children's books—
teaching the police their business. Now, what's all
this about murder? Poor little Hilda. Couldn't have
happened to a nicer person. But what's it to you?
Why haven't all the papers been on it? Nothing's
been said in the *Guardian*.'

'Hilda was a friend of mine,' said Greg. 'We palled
up as soon as I moved to Oswaldston. I think she was
killed, but the police have officially accepted the
death as accidental.'

'I see. You're on to something suspicious, is that it?
Found a vital clue. But *are* you really on to anything,
though? It's not just Enid Blyton stuff, is it?'

'I don't know,' admitted Greg, slightly nettled by
his tone. 'There's very little to go on. But I think she
was killed.'

'You do, eh? Sad about that. Chirpy little body.'
Then, as a new thought struck him and seemed to
give him great delight: 'And you think I did it, eh? Is

that it? You came down here to accuse me of murder, eh?'

'It's not quite like that,' said Greg carefully. 'I came down to get things straight. I thought you were a possibility—you *are* a possibility. But I couldn't see *why* you should—'

'This demands another drink, my boy. This has made my day. It's something at seventy-four to be accused of murder. Hold everything while I get more beer.' And he pottered off to the kitchen in a lather of self-congratulation.

When he got back he was still in a state of high good-humour. Greg, on the other hand, having tried desperately to get his thoughts in order, still felt horribly at sea. Gerald set down the glasses on the table as if he were savouring one of his greatest triumphs.

'Now—down to business! I suppose you want to ask me all the questions they ask in books, eh?'

'Well,' said Greg, 'I suppose I could ask you what you were doing on the night of the eighteenth of May.'

Gerald chuckled. 'And a long way that will get us! I am retired, you know. Not much doing in my life these days—one day very like the next. About all I get asked to do is the occasional lecture. . . . I say, *what* date was it?' He leant across the desk and seized his diary. 'The eighteenth. There you are—wiped off the suspect list in one fell swoop. How depressing! I was asked to give a talk to the Borrowdale Bookman's League. "The D. H. Lawrence Country"—one of my standards. There you are! I'm a wash-out!' He sounded fearfully disappointed.

'It's only an entry in a diary,' said Greg. 'You may not have given the lecture.'

'Ah, quite right.' He brightened up. 'I know what I'll do.' Seizing the phone, and consulting his diary, he rang a number. 'Ah, Mrs Wriothesley? Nice to

hear your voice. Gerald Seymour-Strachey here. . . .
Yes, I enjoyed the visit immensely myself. Such a
pleasant, interested group. But look, there's something arisen here about that—a young man would
like to—check up on my movements, you know?
Nothing important—purely a personal matter. I wonder if you could talk to him about it, eh? Just a
minute, I'll put him on.'

Floundering badly, Greg went though a routine of
questioning: *was* Professor Seymour-Strachey in Borrowdale on the evening of the eighteenth? Yes, he
was. Was Mrs Wriothesley sure it was he? Had she
seen him before? Yes she was. Yes she had. He was
conscious all the time that Mrs Wriothesley was under the impression that he was a suspicious husband
or lover—and that that was precisely the impression
she had been intended to get. When he put down the
phone Gerald Seymour-Strachey was in ecstasies of
lordly self-satisfaction.

'Marvellous, m'boy. You sounded very young. I'm
sure she was enormously impressed. I say—I'll offer
them my "Great Lovers In Literature" lecture next
year. They'll jump at it!'

Greg sat down, depressed. 'I was never that convinced,' he said feebly. 'I couldn't see what motive
there could be.'

'Quite,' said Gerald. 'I've never had a penny out of
those books since Walter died, you know. I suppose I
could have screwed some out of Viola as the price of
keeping quiet, but I never fancied doing it. She's not
the type to put pressure on. I thought she could regard it as a sort of alimony. *I'd* be better off if the
hoax was revealed. That's what I always looked forward to. Lots of fun—interviews, articles and so on.
I'd enjoy it. But I couldn't do that to Viola. I'll just
have to imagine it being revealed after my death.

Melancholy satisfaction, m'boy— melancholy satisfaction!'

Greg found Gerald Seymour-Strachey's poses rather wearing. Together, he and Viola must have been one of the great theatrical partnerships of the century. He said despondently:

'I seem to be back where I started.'

'Can you tell me about it, m'boy? Nothing hush-hush about it, is there?'

'Oh no—not really. I've done nothing I'd want to cover up—except make a damned fool of myself, perhaps.'

'A thought occurs to me,' said Gerald, with an expression of the simplest sort of greed on his face. 'Can you cook?'

'Well, certainly—if it's nothing complicated.'

'I have some pork chops in the fridge, but to be honest I'm not sure what one does with them. And potatoes—I've never understood potatoes, now. Would that be complicated, I wonder?'

'Not unduly,' said Greg, suppressing a smile.

'Then why don't we have a meal? You can cook, and tell me about it while you're doing it.'

So Greg cooked a meal, watched avidly by Gerald Seymour-Strachey, who kept saying things like 'fascinating', and 'terribly clever', until finally he pottered off and opened a bottle, which was something he could do. While this was going on, Greg told him about the case: of the relationship between Hilda and Viola; Viola's attempt to shut Hilda up; the beavering activities of Mr Kronweiser; the row on the night of the fire; the fire in the attic and the supposedly accidental death of Hilda Machin. He added as a *bonne bouche* the information that Viola was slowly driving her daughter-in-law insane, and that Hilda's daughter seemed to be having an affair with the younger Seymour-Strachey. He ended his recital as they were sitting down to table—an immense meal, since Greg suspected that Gerald was really very hungry indeed.

For some minutes there was silence, except for the noise of voracious eating.

'That was fascinating,' said Gerald at last, wiping his mouth in preparation for another descent on his plate. 'Fascinating. Especially as most of the people might be considered my own family! Hilary and Hilda's daughter, eh? I always said he was my son. Not that it would be any different if he were really Walter's!'

'The difficulty is motives. So far as I can see the discovery of the hoax has got me nowhere, and I'm back with the same old one: jealousy and a desire to stop Hilda's mouth as far as Viola is concerned; money as far as the rest are concerned.'

'I'm sure my eldest would do most things for money,' said Gerald dispassionately. 'But I'm not sure it would extend to murder. He's a cautious, cold-blooded little sod. He's the one I can hardly recognize as mine. Viola is much more my idea of a murderer. . . . Banked passions, m'boy, banked passions. An exciting woman, I'll say that for her. There aren't many like her these days. Still, she's a bit wobbly on her pins, isn't she?'

'Yes she is. Very slow and heavy.'

'You'd have difficulty convincing a jury she could scramble up to the attic and start the fire.' Gerald put his knife and fork down for an interval of mastication, and looked thoughtfully at Greg. 'I'm not happy about that fire. A fire to cover a murder. Would anybody actually risk anything so chancy, if they'd really thought it out in advance? Don't you think you might be looking at the whole thing the wrong way round?'

Greg looked at him with slowly dawning comprehension:

'You mean that the main thing was the fire? The destruction of the Machin papers? With the murder of Hilda nothing but an afterthought?'

'It's a possibility, m'boy, isn't it?'

The two sat for a little in thought.

'If that were so,' said Greg slowly, 'there are really only two possibilities. Two people might want to destroy them, to preserve the secret of the hoax. One is Viola—but the same objections apply. The other, I suppose, is Kronweiser.'

'Exactly. Nasty little tyke, as you described him.'

'Oh, he's that all right, and more. And I've considered him, don't think I haven't. When I realized he'd been investigating the phoney letter—'

'Ah, he'd had suspicions, had he?'

'Yes. He'd taken one of the letters Hilda faked over Walter's signature to have the date of the typewriter checked. But it was all right—she wasn't so green, our Hilda. It was only later that I found out a detail was wrong—she'd had Walter see the King and Queen drive past, when in fact they were in America.'

'If you found that out, you can be sure Kronweiser would have checked that too. He's an American researcher—thorough as hell. Just get them on to talking about their research topic and you'll realize that—you've never heard anything as boringly exhaustive as they are. If Kronweiser had doubts, he'd have checked everything in that letter that could be checked. He'd have gone to biographies, newspapers, court circulars.'

'But think—what an inadequate motive! He finds out there are fraudulent letters from the author he's working on. He kills the woman who has been writing them.'

'But you've got it wrong. You didn't stop with the letters—why should he?'

'OK. He found out the author he was working on

was a literary hoax. Instead of exposing it, he burnt
all the papers and killed the person most likely to expose the hoax.'

'Exactly.'

'But it's inadequate. Murder, for a little thing like
that.'

'You're *wrong*, m'boy,' said Gerald, excitedly, shov-
elling the last of his meal into his mouth and pouring
another glass of wine. 'It's the best motive you've got,
by far. You don't *know* these people. You don't *know*
what the academic situation is like in the States. It's
always been publish or perish, but in the last few
years the competition has become fantastically cut-
throat. Thousands of Ph.Ds in the dole queues—just
like cotton-workers in the 'thirties. You've no idea
what you have to do to get jobs in the universities
there these days. We've had Fulbright Professors over
here—their families practically have to make an ap-
pointment to see them for half an hour on Thursdays
and Sundays. Scribble, scribble, scribble. Notes here,
queries there; they think up an idea for an article,
and then they stretch it to three articles. You've got
to have a list of publications as long as your arm before they'll even look at you for what they call "tenure". Otherwise your contract's renewable every
year—and if you let up, it's the boot for you, and
you're lucky if you scrape a job with some Black
Methodist Ladies College somewhere in the deep
South. I tell you, it's *murder*.'

His passion had half-way convinced Greg, but he
still frowned in puzzlement. 'All right, I take your
point. But why not make your reputation and get
your book published by writing an *exposure* of the
hoax?'

'Because that would be nowhere near as satisfactory
as perpetuating it. Look at it from this Kronweiser's
point of view. He exposes the hoax: a nine days' won-

der, congratulations—then what? He's done a year's work on a non-author. Useless! Then look what happens if the lid is kept on the hoax. He is editor of the works and author of the first critical book on an author of major interest. An endless stream of minor articles and reviews pours from his pen. Everything on working-class literature in this century is sent to be subjected to the Kronweiser scrutiny. He's the expert! He's got a corner in a growing literary commodity. His college is proud of him. He's made! It's a hell of a difference, boy. Just a hell of a difference.'

'I'm beginning to see,' said Greg. 'I'm not saying you're not right. But enough to murder for?'

'Surely,' said Gerald. 'And is the murder the main point? That was to burn the manuscripts. The bulk of the evidence—including those forged letters—goes up in smoke. They could have been tested to find out *when* they were typed. Now there are only the copies of Kronweiser's transcripts—not damaging at all. I'll bet you before long he's back in England and removes the telltale one from Jackson's file. Right, then—imagine him waiting on the landing to make sure the thing was well and truly alight. Hilda Machin comes out of her room, starts to run—and he clocks her and leaves her. What was there on the landing?'

'A chair, a table—a lot of bric-à-brac.'

'There you are—the instrument to hand. Probably the chair, I'd say. Quite likely she didn't even see him there. And after the forging of the letters he must have seen Hilda as the main menace. He may even have thought she wrote the books.'

'If he's as smart and thorough as you say, he won't think that for long,' said Greg. 'I think it might be as well for you to be careful. If he suspects . . . It's easier the second time, they say.'

'What about you? Does he know you've been snooping around?'

'Not as far as I know, but could be. Things get around in Oswaldston.'

'Then I'd watch out for yourself too.'

'I'm not worried about that,' said Greg. 'But—what if you are right?'

'I'm damn sure I'm right.'

'What about proving it? What sort of a case could I possibly make?'

'You want to see him tried?'

'Yes,' said Greg determinedly. 'Call me priggish, and upright, and all the rest—but I do. I liked Hilda. If you want me to be primitive. I want to see him punished. I want to hear him squeal.'

'You sound so old-fashioned,' murmured Gerald. 'This business of making a case, though, is not my field. It doesn't sound promising. You said he wasn't around any longer, didn't you?'

'No—he's gone back to the States.'

'You'd have to have a good case to get a warrant for extradition, wouldn't you?'

'Don't I know it. Practically watertight. And what chance is there of that? The police won't even consider the possibility of its being murder.'

'Has there been any talk of arson?'

'No. There was no evidence—but then, that wasn't suspected either, except by me. The insurance company might have gone into it more, but your son's one of the local men.'

'Then they'll pay up generously and ask no questions, you can be sure of that. What else might you do?'

'There's the question of opportunity. Prove he was not at home, that he was seen in the area of the fire after it had started. But where does that get me? His work was there. He had every right to be in the vicinity. He used to go snuffling round the area, soaking up atmosphere. I'd have to prove he was there, that he lit the match, that he bashed Hilda over the head. I don't see a snow-flake's chance in hell of doing it now.'

Gerald pondered a little. 'Tell me,' he said: 'are you interested in getting the case to court and being patted on the back and called a smart boy, or are you interested in justice being done?'

'I'm interested in justice being done.'

'Funny. It's not an abstraction that's ever much appealed to me. Well, it occurs to me that you will, inevitably, see that—if you can wait long enough.'

'How?'

'Justice takes many forms, doesn't it? Think of President Nixon. Just think what's going to happen to this man. He'll go home. The Machin books will be published. His book on Walter will be published. He'll become the Machin expert—deferred to, quoted. He'll get his Associate Professorship, he'll be looking around for a full chair. He'll be throwing himself at the really good universities. And all the time he'll be wondering. Then he'll be waiting. He's burnt his boats —he's lost the option of exposing the hoax by becoming the "expert". And it gradually comes to him that it's only a matter of time before his whole career will collapse in ridicule. People are going to bust a gut laughing at this pompous little ass who's put his shirt on a wooden horse.'

'Why should he fear the hoax will be exposed?'

'Because it's bound to be, sooner or later. He won't be allowed the last word, however polysyllabic his last word is. When you get a writer who's rediscovered, the researchers descend on him like locusts. Eventually someone's going to look at the records—the only things he can't destroy. They're going to look at the marriage certificate. Not conclusive perhaps—written

some years before the books. Then they're going to
look at the *will*. Like you. They're going to see how he
struggles to write his own name—years after the books
are supposed to have been written. And nothing like
his signature on the contracts. And then they're going
to *know*.'

'I wish I could be sure you were right.'

'It'll happen. I know the racket. And there's another thing. We said just now we both weren't safe
from him. There's one way of being a little bit safer:
have a record of the hoax, a full account, safe somewhere, that we could threaten him with. I've been
thinking of writing it myself anyway. It would give
me a lot of satisfaction, and pass the time now I'm
al—while the little lady's away. I'll deposit it at my
bank, for publication when I die. Give me a chuckle
as I'm going, eh? If the whole thing hasn't been exposed by then, you can be sure it will be soon after.'

Greg thought. 'It's an idea,' he said. 'You could say
it's a kind of justice.'

'It's the worst thing that could happen to him.
Can't you see it? Plodding his way up the ladder, step
by laborious step. And all the time waiting—knowing
that there's this bloody great sword over his head,
hanging by a thread. And he'll *know* it's going to fall,
sooner or later. It'll be the purest form of slow tor-
ture. Doesn't the idea appeal to you?'

'Yes,' said Greg slowly. 'I rather think it does.'

Match wits with Richard Jury of Scotland Yard.
And solve these clever thrillers by